Amazon reviews for
'Living I

GW00646323

This book is one of the best I have read. The honesty, love, laughter and tears all captured in one brilliant read.

An excellent read. Touching, humorous, loving; it describes what only those parents closely associated with autism go through. For those of us who are not familiar with autism, it was an eye-opener in showing the stresses and strains, but also the love and rewards that can come with it.

It is full of honesty, humour but most of all love and respect with seemingly getting little in return. Everyone should read this book, whether touched by autism or not. It would help to make us all more tolerant and accepting of those that are a little bit different.

I loved this book! As a parent of two autistic people myself, I can assure would-be readers that the life described by Denis Deasy in this entertaining tale is spot on!

Amazon reviews for
'I'm Sorry, My Son's Autistic'

What an amazing follow up to 'Living in Harry's World' joining Harry and his dad on a heart-warming but rollercoaster of a ride into adulthood. The author really opened my eyes to the world of autism and is a very humbling read. Fantastic read that I couldn't put down. I can't wait until the next instalment.

Author Denis Deasy brilliantly conveys the pressures of dealing with stressful behavioural issues by injecting a degree of humour which is not only entertaining but also gives the reader some insights into the realities of living with autism. I laughed out loud at times and had a tear in my eye at others. This follow-up is highly recommended.

The relationship between Harry and his father is so moving. I loved the many funny incidents and anecdotes - based on Harry's view of the world. A very honest, yet uplifting, account of life with an autistic teenager.

To Susanne and Andrew,

I hope you enjoy the last of the Harry trilogy. I look forward to the day when we can all meet up for a drink. Take care,

Denis Deasy

From This Day Forward

Denis Deasy

Grosvenor House Publishing Limited

The right of Denis Deasy to be identified as the author of this
work has been asserted in accordance with Section 78
of the Copyright, Designs and Patents Act 1988

The book cover is copyright to Denis Deasy
Denis Deasy on Twitter: @DeasyDenis

This book is published by
Grosvenor House Publishing Ltd
Link House
140 The Broadway, Tolworth, Surrey, KT6 7HT.
www.grosvenorhousepublishing.co.uk

This book is a work of fiction. Any resemblance to
people or events, past or present, is purely coincidental.

A CIP record for this book
is available from the British Library

ISBN 978-1-83975-441-8

To all those anonymous, compassionate and non-judgmental people who my son James has approached and scared to death in various towns, cities and countries over the years. Your kindness and tolerance means more to us than you could ever know. Such acts not only reduce our anxiety but also restores our faith in human nature.

Acknowledgement

My thanks to Sean Poole, Noreen Keane and Joanmarie for your taking the time to read my story and your unfailing encouragement. My special thanks to Tony Prouse and Joanna Rees, who both meticulously edited my book; I am so grateful for your kindness and support.

CHAPTER ONE

After waiting for over an hour the waiting room door finally opens and in walks Doctor Rickman and his two colleagues. They sit opposite us.

'Harry is on the autistic spectrum,' Doctor Rickman immediately tells me. There is no room for small talk.

Those six words changed my life forever.

Twenty-six years ago, my son Harry and myself visited Guys hospital in London for a series of tests to determine if he was autistic.

He was and will be for the rest of his life.

Harry was always very different to his peers. At his nursery school he was insular, showing no interest in the other kids. If they tried to interact with him he would inevitably give them a whack. We were always getting phone calls from the nursery school informing us of the latest Harry incident. On some occasions the parents of Harry's victims would call around to our house to remonstrate with us.

Those early years of Harry's life were so stressful. My wife Laura and I were living on the edge every single day. Although most of these memories are still so painful, I find myself recalling those days more frequently of late. Maybe this reflective mood is due to the fact that Harry is approaching his thirtieth birthday and in a few weeks' time will be getting married to his long-term girlfriend Bernadette.

I am waiting in my car for Harry. He lives in a Croydon residential placement for adults with special needs. He stays there Monday to Friday and I have him back for the weekend. I still struggle with the fact that he's not with me during the week even though he's been living away for nearly fourteen years. By the time Friday comes around I am so excited to see him again. Conversely, I have never got over that depressing feeling every Sunday afternoon when I have to drop him back.

My life now is very different from those early years when I didn't have a clue what was going on with Harry. I knew very little about autism then but I've had a crash course on it ever since that fateful day.

When did his unusual behaviour begin to unravel? My mind drifts back to when Harry was three years old.

CHAPTER TWO: 1994

Mrs Hamilton, the head of Harry's latest nursery school approaches us. She looks serious but that seems to be her natural disposition.

'A bad day?' I ask.

She hands me a sheet of paper detailing the various incidents involving Harry. I hand it over to Laura.

'We're going through a difficult time with him right now,' I say.

'Mister McCarthy, there's no such thing as a bad child, it's bad parenting.'

'You're a cruel woman and talking absolute bullshit. I'm glad that I found that out sooner rather than later,' I reply.

With that I take Harry's hand and storm out of the nursery school with Laura trailing behind us.

By the time we get into our car Laura is wiping her tears away.

'I know it's not nice to hear that, but she's a nasty bitch. That place wasn't right for Harry,' I tell her.

After a couple of failed nurseries we had dropped Harry off at this new nursery for them to assess him. It didn't go well.

'He was only there a few hours and in that time he still fought with another child and smeared his shit on several of the toys. Just where do we go from here?' Laura asks.

'I've no idea.'

The fact that Harry's still wearing nappies is an issue for all the nurseries, with the added bonus that for the past twelve months he loves to smear his excrement wherever he likes. This doesn't go down well in a school environment.

'Maybe she's right, we've made mistakes,' Laura adds.

'Don't talk like that. All first time parents make mistakes, it's a learning curve. Harry's a difficult child but he'll come good, I'm sure of that.'

Laura looks at me with such sad eyes.

'Tomorrow I'll try to toilet train him,' I tell my wife, as we arrive home.

I recently purchased a book that claims to toilet train the most disabled of children.

'It won't work. Nothing has so far.'

Without saying a word I take Harry's hand and lead him to the bathroom for his nightly wash.

'It must get better,' I mutter to myself as Harry climbs into the bathtub.

CHAPTER THREE

'Why do I have to get married in a church? I want to get married outside Sainsbury's in Croydon,' Harry asks, seconds after getting into my car.

'We're Catholics and you're getting married in a Catholic church. We're going to see the priest tomorrow, OK?'

'Is that the bloke in black?'

'Correct.'

'Does he like Goofy?'

'I'm not sure.'

'If he doesn't then he can't marry us.'

'Did you have a good week?' I ask, in a vain attempt to change the conversation.

'Do they have burgers and chips at the church?' Harry inquires.

'No, the church is a place of worship, there's no food involved.'

'Sounds like a craphole.'

I sometimes wonder what my relationship would be like if my thirty-year-old son was not autistic. I don't think we'll be talking about whether the priest likes Goofy or the lack of burgers and chips at the church.

'Are you excited about getting married?'

'Twenty-two percent excited. I love the bit when the priest says if anyone can show just cause why this couple cannot lawfully be joined together in matrimony, let them speak now or forever hold their peace.'

'Why do you like that?'

'Cos it's in Shrek. But if anyone objects I'll stick their head down the toilet bowl.'

'I don't think that's said anymore at weddings.'

'It has to be, it's Bernadette's favourite bit as well. I'll have a word with that bloke who's always talking about Jesus.'

'That's the priest and he's a very religious man so you have to show him respect.'

'But he just can't stop talking about Jesus, has he got OCD?'

'No he hasn't.'

Not that I'm aware of anyway.

'But how can I respect a man who doesn't like Goofy? It doesn't make any sense.'

'So what do you want to do tonight?'

'Is the Irish chick at home?'

'No, Kerry's at her mothers.'

'Is she staying there until her mother drops dead?'

'Bridget's only got flu so she'll be OK.'

'That flu lady looks like King Kong.'

'That's not nice, why do you say that?'

'She's fat and hairy.'

Bridget could do with losing a few pounds (can't we all?) and perhaps she has a slight growth above her lips, but that alone doesn't deserve the King Kong comparison.

'Nineteen days ago I told her that as well.'

'And what did she say?' I nervously ask.

'She just stared at me. I don't think she understood. She speaks another language.'

My mother-in-law is Irish and from my understanding knows about three Gaelic words, but that's enough for Harry to believe that she doesn't understand English.

'Are you finished talking about Bridget?'

'Does she go to the toilet?'

'What do you mean?'

'I don't think she does. Her face is a bulging red as if she's desperate to have a shit, but can't. My face is always red before a crap but afterwards it's pink.'

'Rest assured she does go to the toilet.'

'Are you sure about that? Have you ever seen her having a shit?'

'OK, let's drop this conversation now.'

I must admit I didn't think I would be talking about my mother-in-law's toiletry habits today.

I have been married to Kerry for twelve years. She has a severely autistic son called Niall through her former husband Danny. Danny left when Naill was eleven. Naill has been to three residential placements for special needs adults in London, all of which didn't work out. Niall is an extremely complex person. He is completely non-verbal and consequently can get frustrated and aggressive. The aggression has lessened over the last few years but his behaviour is unpredictable. Two years ago Kerry found an excellent residential placement in Brighton for Niall, but she couldn't bear to be away from her son so she rented a place down there about eighteen months ago. She also got a new teaching job a few minutes' walk from Niall's new 'home'. Although Brighton isn't a million miles away from my Streatham house we don't get to see a lot of each other. Her weekends are spent with Niall and mine with Harry. We get together as often as we can, but there's no question it has put a strain on our marriage. Kerry was due to spend this weekend with me but her elderly mother fell ill so she decided to look after her for a couple of days.

As I'm driving home I pull over to let an ambulance through.

'Wow, that guy's driving way too fast,' Harry says.

'He's got to take a sick person to the hospital and has to get there as quickly as possible.'

'I'm fed up of ambulances not stopping at red lights. I'm going to ring the cops.'

'Do *not* phone the police, OK?'

'But those shits are driving like crazy.'

'There's someone in the ambulance that needs urgent medical attention and that's why they're going fast,' I re-iterate.

'But everyone apart from those ambulance bastards stop at red lights, so they should as well. When the lights turn amber then they can get ready to go and when they're green they can drive off.'

I get the concept.

'What do you want to do tonight?' I ask again.

'I want to meet one of those celebrities.'

'Which one?'

'Any American actor, cos they smile better than our lot. Do they have smile classes in their American schools?'

'No, I don't think so.' But what do I know?

'So have you any idea which celebs you want to meet?'

'Jim Carrey or Tom Hanks. Are they in Streatham today?'

'That's unlikely.'

'Is it because Streatham's a dump?'

'No, they're probably in Hollywood making films.'

'Oh alright. Can I buy a horse? Do they sell them on eBay?' Harry asks, the master at changing the subject.

Probably.

'That's out of the question.'

'But I want to ride the horse through the shopping mall and tie it up outside Sainsbury's when I go to get my Kit Kats. Do horses like Kit Kats?'

'No they don't.'

'What about twirls?'

'Harry, we're not getting a horse, OK? Now what do you want to do tonight?'

'I need to have a massive crap.'

So after discussing my mother-in-law's mortality, ambulances driving through red lights, Americans being taught to smile at school and purchasing a horse on eBay, we are on our way home so Harry can go to the toilet.

I do remember very clearly spending a whole day with Harry with the sole purpose of toilet training him.

CHAPTER FOUR: 1994

'What am I going to do for eight hours?' Laura asks.

'Just go shopping or run a marathon; I don't care. I just need to have the whole day with Harry,' I reply.

'I really think this is a waste of time.'

'Maybe, but I'm willing to give it a try.'

Laura kisses Harry on the forehead and leaves without acknowledging me.

Harry's toilet issues are proving extremely stressful and stopping him from getting into any nursery school. He just loves to smear his excrement everywhere – on the furniture, carpets, walls, bed linen, computer and TV screens – practically everywhere apart from inside the toilet bowl.

Today I am going through all the exercises in the book that claims to toilet train the most disabled of people. I can but hope that it will work for my son.

I take off Harry's nappies and give him savoury snacks like crisps and peanuts followed by several cups of water. As per the book instructions I do this at various parts of the house and we then make a dash to the toilet. After nearly three hours of this activity Harry finally pees into the toilet for the first time ever. I feel absolutely elated. This may seem a little over the top but this is a massive step forward and going to make our life so much easier.

I continue giving him snacks and water and a couple of hours later he pees again. I jump up in the air as if I've just scored the winning goal in the World Cup Final. Harry just stares at me.

I had purchased some special dolls and a miniature plastic toilet and in between all this activity I show Harry several times how to pee and poo into the toilet using the dolls.

After seven and a half hours I finally give up with only half of my two targets successfully achieved. I venture into the kitchen to prepare the dinner and it isn't long before I can smell something very familiar. The TV in the living-room is covered in excrement and it's all on Harry's hands. I close my eyes and start to cry.

A few minutes later Laura arrives home.

'Didn't work then?' She asks as she enters the living-room.

'He did pee in the toilet a couple of times.'

'OK, that's a start. Well done, Harry.'

I detect a disappointed tone in her voice which surprises me as she seemed to have zero expectations that any of this would work, but I'm also frustrated as the smearing of his poo is causing us all the problems at the nursery school and at home.

However, little did I know as I'm disinfecting the TV that the next day Harry pooed into the toilet and never smeared his shit ever again.

CHAPTER FIVE

We're in our local Italian restaurant. These are the times I enjoy the best; just the two of us.

The waiter approaches our table.

'Are you ready to order?' He asks.

'Are you the same crowd that made that shit food on the aeroplane when we went to Italy last year?' Harry inquires.

'No, we don't provide the plane food.'

'OK, Harry, what do you want to eat?' I ask my son.

'Have you got any food that's *not* Italian?'

The waiter stares at Harry and then glances over at me.

'My son's autistic,' I say to him.

He immediately smiles at me.

'What would you like to eat?' He asks Harry.

'Steak and kidney pie, chips and mushy peas.'

'OK, I can arrange that,' he replies, probably thinking of popping over to the fish and chip shop a few doors down.

'Why the hell are you insulting the Italians?' I say, after ordering my lasagne.

'They talk way too fast.'

I decide not to pursue this conversation.

'So have you decided who's going to be your best man?' I ask my son.

'It's a shame that Bruce Forsyth's dead, cos I would've definitely asked him.'

That makes me feel so much better.

'The wedding's only three weeks away, you must make your mind up soon.'

'I did send a letter to Lee Mack.'

'The comedian?'

'Yes.'

'Did he reply?'

'Not yet.'

'Why did you choose him?'

'He makes me laugh, although he's not really funny when he has that beard.'

It seems that the essential credentials to be a best man is to be alive, clean shaven and funny. I tick the first two boxes and maybe the third, after a couple of glasses of wine, but I'm still not in the running.

I'm actually feeling quite depressed that Harry hasn't asked me. Maybe he doesn't fully understand how important it is. I'm clinging onto that theory.

I cannot believe that Harry is getting married. I just never thought that it would ever happen. Bernadette is a lovely girl and perfect for Harry. I've never seen them argue. I don't think a 'normal' girl would tolerate Harry and his ways. I don't know what the statistics are for relationships between autistic and 'normal' people but at a guess I would think it would be quite low. Having said that I'm assuming that in autistic male/female relationships it isn't that common either, that's why I am thrilled for Harry that he's found someone. I suppose I'm no different from any other parent.

'Is Bernadette looking forward to seeing the priest tomorrow?' I ask.

'No.'

'Why not?'

'She doesn't like all the different colours in the church windows.'

'But they're beautiful stained glass windows from medieval times.'

'She doesn't recognise the person in the window.'

'It's Jesus.'

'Him again?'

'Harry, what have I told you a million times about being disrespectful to the church?'

'But why can't they have a Lee Mack window; without the beard?'

I have spent the last month talking to Social Services about Harry and Bernadette sleeping together once they got married as they have to give it the OK, which they have. However, I haven't yet discussed this with Harry, but no time like the present.

'Jerry said that you'll be sharing a bed with Bernadette after you get married. Are you looking forward to that?'

'If she snores I'll tell her to sleep in the corridor.'

Making a relationship work is all about compromise isn't it?

'You've never shared a room with anyone before, do you feel nervous about it?'

'Although she loves my Thomas DVDs she wants to line them up in alphabetic order but I always have them in date order. That's going to be a problem.'

'Anything else that concerns you?'

'Batman.'

'What do you mean?'

'Adam West is the best Batman ever. He was in 128 episodes from 1966 to 1968. I loved it when he kicked that shark in the face and then killed him with the anti-shark repellent spray in the 1966 film.'

'Why is that an issue?'

'Bernadette thought that the shark was only trying to kiss Batman's leg and that Batman didn't need to kick the shark's face.'

She didn't seem bothered then that Batman eventually killed the shark!

'Does she like all the other actors who play Batman?'

'No, but I don't either.'

'Will you be going to bed at the same time as Bernadette?'

Harry is extremely particular in his sleeping arrangements. He nearly always goes to bed at five minutes past nine. Getting to sleep is another matter as he tends to watch his DVDs for a few hours before nodding off.

'No, she goes to bed at 9:45 and wants to go to sleep straight away.'

What a novel concept.

'But there's no way that's going to stop me watching my DVDs.'

So the future of their relationship depends on coming to an agreement on how to line up Harry's DVDs, accepting a difference of opinion on Adam West and whether Bernadette can sleep when Harry plays his Thomas DVDs in bed. Slightly different issues to most other married couples.

Since Harry was a baby, sleeping has always been an issue. In fact it was one of the reasons that led to Laura's breakdown that in turn led to the end of our marriage.

CHAPTER SIX: 1994

'I've got a big day at work today, can't you see to him?' I ask Laura.

'I did it yesterday.'

'Yeah, for the first couple of hours and then I took over.'

'I *need* to sleep; just *do it*.'

I make my way downstairs to find Harry in our garden throwing my Elton John LPs into my neighbour's garden. I manage to stop him before I lose *Goodbye Yellow Brick Road*.

'Get in *now*!' I shout at my son.

It's quarter past one in the morning. I'm sure that the neighbours are now familiar with our night time antics.

Harry can get by with only a couple of hours sleep and maybe catch up with a nap during the day. Unfortunately, I don't have that luxury at work. This sleep deprivation has been happening since Harry was born. It's like living with a new born baby for the past three years.

'Let's go to bed,' I plead.

'No sleep.' Harry defiantly responds.

I try to guide him upstairs but he refuses to move. On some nights I lift him up and lay him down in his bed, but this never works because only a few minutes later he makes his way downstairs.

'Thomas video,' he tells me.

Reluctantly I put on a Thomas video in the living-room. He has a TV and video recorder in his bedroom and he refuses to watch anything there. It has to be in the living-room.

Harry puts on a *Thomas The Tank Engine* video and sits on the floor in front of the TV. Although he's seen this video a hundred times he's still transfixed by it.

Knowing that I'm here for the long haul I make myself a cup of tea and plonk myself down in the armchair. I don't want to fall asleep as this gives Harry the perfect excuse to go searching for goodies. I once caught him opening up a packet of paracetamol at two o'clock in the morning. That petrified me. Now all of the medicines are kept under lock and key.

I don't dare start reading as that will inevitably send me to sleep, so I sit through the less than enthralling Thomas video.

'Come on, Harry, it's time for bed,' I say after the video has finished.

Harry just ignores me and puts in *The Little Mermaid* video.

I switch off the TV and gently attempt to pull Harry up by his arms, but he's having none of it and gives me a kick in the shins in protest.

'That hurt,' I shout at my son, but he switches the TV back on and stares at the opening credits of *The Little Mermaid*.

I know whatever I try I'm not going to win this battle so reluctantly I settle back in the armchair to view the video for the umpteenth time. I nod off after about half an hour and when I wake up again at three minutes past four Harry is watching another Thomas video. He's looking tired so I turn off the TV and this time my shins escape another attack.

I guide Harry upstairs to his room and set the alarm for five-thirty and as usual I lay down alongside him.

It's going to be another tough day at work.

CHAPTER SEVEN

'I want to drive to Southend-On-Sea to see Kerry this morning,' I say to Harry.

'That's going to take one hour and thirty minutes by car to get there and about one hour and thirty minutes to get back. That's wasting my time.'

'Harry, Kerry's my wife, I have to see her.'

'Just get another wife instead, then we don't have to make that crap journey. There's plenty of wives in Streatham.'

'As soon as you've had your bath and get changed we're going to Southend-On-Sea; OK?'

'But the beaches there are full of stones. What's all that about? Did they sell all the sand to the bloke who owns Bournemouth?'

Before I have a chance to reply Harry speaks again.

'And those fucking seagulls are evil bastards. I saw them fly down and grab a couple of chips off some old bloke and he didn't even tell them off. Maybe the seagulls were his pets? They scare the shit out of me.'

As the traffic was heavy it takes us just over two hours to reach Southend-On-Sea.

'We're thirty-two minutes late. You fucked it up again,' Harry says as we approach Bridget's house.

'No, I didn't, there was a lot of traffic.'

'But the internet said it will take one hour and thirty minutes and it took us two hours and two minutes. You really are a shit driver. Have you taken your driving test yet?'

'Yes, I took it in 1981.'

'But that's a few centuries ago. You must have forgotten how to drive since then.'

'Harry, we're here now.'

'But the internet said…'

'Forget what the fucking internet said,' I shout at my son.

I glance up and see my mother-in-law standing at her doorway.

'How are you feeling now?' I ask her, feeling somewhat embarrassed.

'All the better for hearing you effing and jeffing.'

'Sorry about that,' I meekly reply.

'Come in, Kerry's just taken Niall to the toilet. And how are you, Harry?'

'Pissed off.'

'Why's that?'

'I'm in this shithole town and where the hell's your carpet gone to?' Harry asks as he enters the front hallway.

'I just had wooden flooring put down. It's so much better.'

'It's way too hard on my feet. I won't be able to get to sleep tonight because of this,' Harry says pointing to the floor.

'Don't worry about it, Harry, you'll be fine. How's your cold?' I ask Bridget.

'It's fine. I don't know why Kerry even bothered to come here, but of course it's always nice to see her and Niall.'

Kerry and Niall came down the stairs to greet us. The hug that Kerry gives me is restrained, especially as it's been three weeks since I last saw her.

Kerry has that distinctive Irish look – long, ginger hair, fair skin with striking green eyes. She's short and slim and still a beautiful woman.

Niall is a good four or five inches taller than her with dark hair and despite his passion for food he remains trim.

'Hello, Harry, how are you?' Kerry asks.

'Fucked off. I thought you said that your mum was going to pop her clogs? She looks like she's still got a couple of weeks to go yet. We came down here for nothing.'

Kerry and Bridget look confused.

'Don't worry, Harry's got the wrong end of the stick,' I explain.

Niall approaches me. He licks my hand and twists my nose.

'Are you OK, Niall?' I ask.

He then takes off one of his shoes and gently taps the top of my head.

Licking, nose twisting and placing a shoe on my head are typical Niall greetings.

'Do you want to watch *Thomas And The Magic Railroad*?' Harry asks Niall holding up his DVD and portable DVD player.

Niall bangs his fist on his forehead, which means that he's either excited or frustrated. This time I think he's excited. He has a huge lump at the top of his forehead due to his constant fist banging. I doubt it'll ever go away.

'Alec Baldwin should've won an Oscar for playing Mr Conductor in *Thomas And The Magic Railroad* but instead those Oscar simpletons gave it to that Spacey bloke for that ridiculous film *American Beauty*. What's all that about? If I was Baldwin I'd sue Oscar,' Harry tells Niall as they walk into the living-room.

'Your mum seems OK, you could've come home,' I say to Kerry.

'She's old now, David. I worry about her.'

'Do you also worry about our marriage?'

'That's not fair.'

'Well it seems to be me who's making all the effort to see you.'

'David, Niall is thriving in his home and I have to be with him at the weekends. You've got to see that?'

It's understandable that Kerry is concerned about her mother, but Bridget just has a mild flu and it seems to me like she's using any excuse not to make that trip to Streatham.

It's obviously less stressful for her not making that journey and just spending her weekends with Niall. Harry and Niall do get on better now than in the past but they're both extremely unpredictable, so when the four of us are together it can be absolute chaos.

Is Kerry choosing an easier life at the expense of our marriage?

'Niall is just so happy in Brighton,' Kerry tells me.

'Of course and I'm genuinely thrilled for him, but we've been living apart for eighteen months and I just can't see how we're going to resolve this.'

Kerry gently rubs my back. 'Let's not talk about this right now.'

I was about to reply when Bridget approaches.

'The boys are settled. I've got some tea and cake in the kitchen. How does that sound?'

We both smile at her and follow her into the kitchen.

As we're chatting, my mind wanders back to my first marriage with Laura. We were together five years before Harry was born. We shared a lot of the same interests, going to concerts, the theatre, holidays abroad etc. They were really happy and carefree years. We always wanted children and talked about having at least two, so when Harry was born we were absolutely thrilled. The early months of Harry not sleeping extended into years and slowly the sleep deprivation and Harry's increasingly strange behaviour began to take its toll on both of us.

CHAPTER EIGHT: 1994

We arrive home from the latest nursery school after hearing another bad report on Harry. This is happening every day now. How much longer can this go on?

'Why's Harry so different to all the other kids in the nursery school? He doesn't interact with any of them and his speech is also behind his peers. I'm worried,' Laura tells me.

'I know, but give it time; he'll catch up,' I reply.

'Are you living in cloud cuckoo land? There's something seriously wrong here, David. Can't you see that?'

'So what do you want to do?'

'I dunno, go to a professional; a doctor or a psychiatrist?'

'Don't you think you're overreacting?'

'No I fucking don't. Harry's different and I can't work out why. He never makes eye contact with us ever and when was the last time you saw him smile?' Laura asks.

'He's a serious boy, that's nothing to be concerned about.'

'He doesn't interact with us at all. Do you think that's normal as well?'

'But the staff at his nursery say that he's just a little slow.'

'What the fuck do they know? They're just child minders, nothing more. I can't take the endless sleepless nights, his unprovoked aggressive behaviour and his total lack of involvement in anything apart from his beloved *Thomas The Tank Engine* videos. It's tearing me apart. I just don't know what to do next.'

'OK, OK, let's go and see that child psychiatrist in Wimbledon that Helen used to see when she was having issues with Charlie. I think her name was Carol. I remember her saying that the sessions were really helpful. Maybe she can unravel some of Harry's behaviours and if nothing else we could get her to write a referral letter for our doctor to take this further.'

'Can you take care of that?' Laura asks, as she wipes away the ever present tears.

'Of course,' I reply as I hold her in my arms.

CHAPTER NINE: TWO WEEKS LATER

I feel nervous as I enter Carol's office and I can tell that Laura is too. I never thought that we would feel the need to visit a psychologist about Harry but we don't know where to turn to next and this seems like a good place to start.

Her office looks more like a living-room, with a two seater sofa and a couple of armchairs.

Carol greets us with warm handshakes. She's tall, very pretty and smartly dressed in a navy blue skirt and jacket. She's younger than I expected, maybe in her early forties.

She beckons us to sit down on the sofa.

'I'm coming into this with very little background so can you tell me your main concerns about Harry?' Carol asks.

'This session's only for an hour so not enough time,' Laura replies.

'He's aggressive. He hits and pinches us both many times during the course of a day. He does the same to the kids at the nursery; he only sleeps a couple of hours a night and when he's up either myself or Laura has to be up as well; and he seems slower than the kids in his class and just doesn't interact with us at all. No eye contact and his speech is well behind his peers. Is that enough to be going on with?' I ask.

Carol nods as she frantically writes down this information.

'What do you want to tackle first?' She asks.

'His aggression,' Laura quickly replies.

'Can you identify any specific occurrences that trigger this aggression?'

'It's extremely random. When we pick him up from nursery he charges towards us like a bull heading for a red rag. He crashes into either me or David, nearly knocking us over. He's constantly pinching us from the moment he wakes up to when he goes to bed. He kicks David in the shins on a daily basis and as you can imagine that must really hurt. We're calm parents so his aggression is not a reaction to us telling him off, it's totally haphazard and that's not normal,' Laura responds.

'And how do *you* react when he hurts you?'

'I tell him off and let him know that it's unacceptable, but he doesn't even look up at me. I really don't think he understands what we're saying to him.'

'There must be a reason why he suddenly starts attacking you both,' Carol proclaims.

'There's no obvious triggers,' Laura replies.

'OK, can you tell me what happens after he wakes up in the morning?'

'He usually has Frosties without milk. Sometimes toast, always with the crusts cut off. When he finishes he nearly always rushes over to me or David and gives us a couple of pinches on the arm.'

'Is it a playful pinch?'

'No it fucking hurts,' Laura angrily replies as she rolls up her sleeves to show the bruises on each arm.

Again Carol nods and continues to write.

'Does he hand back his empty breakfast bowl to you?'

'No, but what's that got to do with anything?'

'Does he tidy up his toys after he plays with them?'

'We always tell him to, but he makes a token effort of putting one or two away and leaves the rest to us.'

'It sounds like he could have oppositional defiant disorder.'

'And what the hell is that?' Laura asks.

'It's abbreviated to ODD. It's when a child displays an ongoing pattern of an angry or irritable mood, defiant or argumentative behaviour, and vindictiveness toward people in authority – for example you and David. Although you could say that some kids of Harry's age display such behaviour when it lasts longer than say six months and is excessive, compared to what is usual for a child of Harry's age, then I'd say it's ODD.'

'Are you sure about this?' I ask.

'No not yet, but I'm going to give you some tests to see how Harry reacts and depending on how he responds will help to clarify my thoughts.'

'And what's the treatment for ODD?'

'Normally it's a couple of drugs like Aripiprazole and Risperidone, but it's way too early to be talking about medication.'

'What sort of tests must we do?' I ask.

'I want you to document on a daily basis how many times he shows defiant behaviour and that could be either hitting or just not picking up toys when asked.

In fact one of my testing methods requires you getting a box, I call it a 'Sunday Box', and with all the toys or videos that he doesn't pick up, you put them in this box and say that he can't access them until the following week.'

'OK we'll give it a go,' Laura replies, although she doesn't sound convinced.

In a strange way I feel relieved that we're able to put a label on some of Harry's behaviour. We've got something to work with.

I leave Carol's office in a much better frame of mind than when I arrived.

CHAPTER TEN

We are waiting outside the church for Bernadette and her mother Alice. We have a meeting with Father Quinlan to discuss the wedding. I have told Harry several times in the past few days not to say anything inappropriate to Father Quinlan, but I suspect he will completely ignore my advice.

'How old is this joint?' Harry asks me.

'This is not a joint, it's a church. I think it's nearly 200 years old.'

'Fuck that, it won't collapse on my head during the wedding, will it?'

'No, it won't.'

'Do I have to wear a bicycle helmet just in case?'

'That won't be required.'

'But I don't want to get my head smashed to little bits when I'm getting married.'

'Don't worry, the church is safe.'

I knew that we couldn't stay too long in Southend-On-Sea as we had to get back here, but as the conversation between myself and Kerry was strained we left a couple of hours earlier than I had originally intended. This ongoing tense relationship is constantly on my mind and there's seemingly no easy resolution to our living situation. What I do know is that if we continue the way things are right now our marriage is doomed to failure.

A few minutes later Bernadette and Alice arrive. Harry approaches Bernadette and kisses her forehead.

'Has the religion man got a beard?' Bernadette asks me.

'No, he's clean shaven,' I reply.

'Does he wear those flare trousers?'

'No, I don't think so.'

'That's good. I hate the way they flap.'

'I don't think you'll see too many people with flares these days.'

'But last week I saw on YouTube loads of people with flares at some music festival from a few centuries ago. They all had hair all over the place,' Bernadette says.

'That was probably in the 1960s and I would imagine that most of those people probably haven't got much hair left now. ' I reply, speaking from personal experience.

'Shall we forget about beards, flares and hair and go and see the priest?' Alice asks.

Harry takes Bernadette's hand as we walk into the church, and although I've seen this many times previously it still makes me smile.

As soon as we enter the church Father Quinlan is there to greet us.

'And how are you today, Harry?' Father Quinlan asks.

'I'm still confused why you don't like Lee Mack?' Harry inquires.

'I'm sorry, I don't understand.'

'You've got Jesus everywhere in this place, but no Lee Mack statues at all, or even on the windows.'

'Harry, what did I say about being rude?' I tell my son.

'But don't you think he's a little too obsessed with Jesus?' Harry replies, pointing to Father Quinlan.

'I'm sorry Father,' I say.

My parents were strict Irish Catholics. They went to Mass every day of the week. If they heard Harry talking like this to a priest they would have gone berserk. Harry and myself go to Mass every Sunday and it's probably the most stressful hour of the week (although there are a number of contenders for this honour). I have tried to bring up Harry to respect the church, but so far I have failed. However, I do pray every day. I always ask for help in making Harry's life better.

'No need to apologise. Yes, you are right, Harry, I am obsessed with Jesus.'

'I told you,' Harry proclaims.

'But that's a good thing. And I do like Lee Mack, but a church isn't the right place for a statue of him. Now is this your wife to be?' Father Quinlan asks, pointing to Bernadette.

'How long does the wedding last for?' Bernadette asks.

'Usually around sixty minutes.'

'That's way too long. I'll be bored out of my brains. Cut it down to ten minutes, OK?'

'Bernadette, please don't be so abrupt to the priest,' Alice tells her daughter.

'I'm afraid it's always going to be about an hour,' Father Quinlan re-iterates.

'Let's go to Vegas, they do it much quicker there,' Harry tells Bernadette.

'A fantastic idea. I bet the religious men there are a lot more fun than this one,' Bernadette replies.

Father Quinlan smiles. 'Well, I don't think I can put on a Vegas spectacular but I can sing a hymn or two'.

Harry and Bernadette look at each other in confusion.

Up to now Harry and Bernadette didn't seem to care how they got married, so as Laura and myself are both Catholics we made the decision on their behalf to get married in a Catholic church. Of course we discussed this with Alice and she was really positive about it. However as the big day is upon us I'm getting increasingly nervous. Will they both be able to cope with the length of the Mass? I guess it won't be long before we find out.

We spend the next forty-five minutes discussing the wedding vows etc. Father Quinlan was very patient with them both especially when Harry asked him if there was enough toilet rolls in the bogs in case he needed to go for a crap during the wedding. Father Quinlan also agreed to say the 'speak now or forever hold your peace' line. Harry and Bernadette both gave him a high five after that. Despite the shaky start to our visit I thought that overall it went well.

'Where's Greg?' I ask Alice on the way out of the church.

'He really wanted to be here but he had too many meetings.'

Greg is Alice's husband and Bernadette's stepfather. One Sunday afternoon many years ago Harry wanted to play the piano at Heathrow airport and he enlisted the help of Bernadette as his backing singer and dancer.

It went down a storm and one of the spectators that day was Greg. He was on his way to Switzerland and came over for a quick chat afterwards. He told myself and Alice how moved he was by their performance, saying that his sister has an autistic boy. Upon his return he contacted Alice and within a year they were married. He's a great guy and has been more of a father to Bernadette than her own dad, Francis. He left when she was ten years old and she'd be lucky to receive birthday or Christmas cards from him.

'I'm surprised Laura's not here,' Alice says.

'She's in Ireland right now. She'll be back tomorrow.'

'Can you believe that our kids are going to get married in a couple of weeks? I never ever thought that Bernadette would be in any sort of a relationship, let alone get married.'

'I know, I feel exactly the same about Harry. I'm excited but also nervous. It's going to be a change of life for them both and us too.'

'Yeah, totally agree. I won't be seeing her as much at the weekends which will be really hard to deal with but it's all for the best. Bernadette's so happy when she's with Harry and that's all that counts.'

I look over to see if Harry or Bernadette can hear our conversation, but they're too busy discussing the type of wood that the church pews are made of.

I wish that Laura was with me today. She's been through so much with Harry that it would have been so lovely for her to see her son and Bernadette discussing their wedding in their own inimitable way with the priest. She would have been in her element but she said that Sean had to go to Ireland urgently so she decided to go with him. It must have been important.

Laura noticed that something was seriously wrong with Harry way before I did. I was in denial. I can remember our second visit to the psychiatrist as if it were yesterday.

CHAPTER ELEVEN: 1994

As we're in Carol's waiting room I notice a woman leaving her office holding a handkerchief. I can clearly see that she's been crying as she walks past us. Laura and I exchange a look but don't say anything. A couple of minutes later we enter Carol's office.

'So tell me how did it go with the Sunday box?' Carol asks us.

'A waste of time,' Laura quickly responds.

'In what way?'

'Well, we told him to pick up all his toys and he made the great effort to pick up just one. We then let him know that we were putting all the other toys that were scattered around into the Sunday box and reminded him that he wouldn't see them for another week.'

'And how did he react?'

'He didn't acknowledge us at all and has been nowhere near the box since. So where do we go from here?'

'That's unusual. I'll have a rethink on that. For the time being let's leave that to one side and move on to his aggression.'

'So are you saying that the ODD diagnosis is now incorrect?' Laura asks.

'No, that would've been just one typical example of ODD. I'm just a little confused why he didn't create a

FROM THIS DAY FORWARD

fuss over those toys, but never mind. Have you got some totals about how many times he assaulted you?'

I hand over a sheet of paper detailing the daily counts.

'Wow, that's averaging about eight to nine attacks for each of you every day. That's a lot. Does he ever say sorry?' Carol asks.

'Never,' I quickly respond.

'Do you try to stop him?'

'Of course, but he's absolutely determined. His eyes seem to glaze over as he's about to attack us. It's almost as if he's in a trance. It's horrendous and scary,' Laura replies.

'Sounds like OCD. He has to fulfil that need and nothing will stop him. Harry's seems an extremely complex child. He has a lot of issues. How are you both coping with it?'

'We hardly ever argued before Harry was born but now it's a daily occurrence. The attacks, the lack of interaction with Harry, and the sleep deprivation has put a great strain on our marriage,' I blurt out.

Laura looks surprised at my admission, but what's the point of attending these sessions if we don't disclose the whole picture?

'That's perfectly understandable. There's a missing link here and I just can't work out what it is yet, but with further sessions I will get to the bottom of it I promise you. Do not despair,' Carol tells us.

'Don't you think that you were a little too aggressive to her?' I ask Laura as we get into our car.

'No, not at all. I'm questioning her methods, there's nothing wrong in that.'

'But it's early days and she's the professional. We've got to give her time.'

'OK, but there's no silver bullet here, just remember that.'

CHAPTER TWELVE

My suggestion of a drink or two was readily accepted by Alice.

'So are we all set up for the wedding?' She asks me as I pour her a glass of wine.

'Pretty much, although he still hasn't picked his best man,' I reply.

'Really? I just assumed it would be you.'

'No, he hasn't asked yet. I've give it until next weekend and then I'll volunteer myself. Not the normal course of events, but needs must.'

'That must be hard for you.'

'Yeah, you could say that.'

'So what date will I have to make an application for a divorce?' Harry asks, as he enters the living-room, accompanied by his wife-to-be.

'What do you mean?' I nervously ask.

'You got rid of mum very quickly and Bernadette's father buggered off as well. I just want to know when it's my turn.'

'That's completely different, it's nothing to do with you and Bernadette. You're going to be very happy together.'

'But that Brighton bird doesn't want to live with you anymore, so are you going to divorce her as well?'

'Don't worry about Kerry, it'll work out,' I reply sounding more confident than I feel.

'See, I told you, Harry. We don't need to get divorced. Let's just get married instead,' Bernadette says.

Alice looks over at me with a relieved expression.

'And Harry wants to play *Crocodile Rock* on the piano when I'm running down the church gangway,' Bernadette adds.

'No, Harry's not playing anything in the church. As per tradition you'll be walking down the aisle to *Here Comes The Bride*,' Alice says.

'But that's so boring. What about *Yellow Submarine*?' Harry asks.

'No, it's still *Here Comes The Bride*,' Alice re-iterates.

'I thought you said that all the details of the wedding were sorted,' Alice informs me with a smile.

'There's a piano at the reception, so you can play *Crocodile Rock* and *Yellow Submarine* there if you like,' I tell my son.

'OK, but the wedding guests will all have to pay a tenner each to hear me sing.'

'We're not charging the wedding guests, OK?'

'But Elton John charges seventy quid to hear him sing *Crocodile Rock* and he doesn't even give the audience pork pies.'

'You still haven't decided where you want to go for a honeymoon. I need to know as I have to take time off work,' I ask, in a deliberate attempt to drift away from the Elton John/pork pies conversation.

'Halifax.'

'You want to go to Halifax for your honeymoon?'

'Yep.'

'And where do you want to go, Bernadette?'

'Halifax.'

'Why the hell do you want to go there?' I ask them both.

'Because it was voted in the top ten worst places to visit in England,' Bernadette replies.

'OK, so that should be a clue as to why you shouldn't go there.'

'We just want to find out how shit it is.'

'What about Los Angeles, New York, Paris or Rome?'

'Nah, it's definitely Halifax. They have a really good McDonalds there and a WH Smiths inside the train station. It's only 213 miles away,' Harry proclaims.

'OK, Halifax it is. I'll look into hotels. Are you coming as well?' I ask Alice.

'Yes, and hopefully Greg. I'll let you know in a couple of days if that's OK?'

'No problem.'

'I'll ask Laura if she wants to come. I'm sure she will.'

As I'm staring at my son I know that in a couple of weeks he will no longer be so dependent on me, even though it seems a whole gang of us will have to accompany him and Bernadette on their honeymoon. Although Harry lives away from me during the week, his comings and goings are still very carefully monitored and controlled by the staff that run his residential home. That's why there is no way he would be allowed to travel and stay in Halifax, even with Bernadette.

I have been living alone with Harry since he was four, when Laura had a nervous breakdown. That was primarily caused by the stress in bringing up Harry. Laura made it quite clear that she wanted to live alone, so I rented a flat in Streatham with Harry. The separation eventually lead to the breakdown of our marriage. In time, Laura recovered and has been trying to make up for it every day since. She is now happily married to Sean and has a wonderful relationship with Harry, but back then things were very different.

CHAPTER THIRTEEN: 1994

'What did he do today?' Laura asks me as I enter our house.

It's five o'clock in the afternoon and she's still in her dressing gown. She doesn't take her eyes off the TV. I look to see what she's watching and it's an episode of *Barney And Friends*, which is not her usual TV viewing. In fact she has told me on several occasions that she would like 'to beat the shit out of that dinosaur' as Harry plays the Barney videos constantly.

'You like Barney now?' I ask her.

She doesn't answer.

Harry comes into the living-room and immediately sits in front of the TV. *Barney And Friends* has now captivated two-thirds of the McCarthy household. Laura doesn't acknowledge Harry's presence.

'In answer to your earlier question, Harry sat in the corner of the classroom throughout the whole of the nursery session, didn't engage in any of the activities and kicked Kevin in the shins because he wore a yellow jumper. I'm afraid he won't last too long there if this continues.'

'So pretty much the same as any other day then,' Laura eventually responds.

'Have you eaten?' I ask.

Laura just stares at the TV. Barney's inane dialogue is obviously more interesting than mine. However, I'm getting used to this one-way conversation.

'Did you make that doctors appointment?' I ask.

Am I totally invisible now?

'Don't worry, I'll ring them tomorrow,' I reply to my own question.

I enter the kitchen to start the dinner and a few minutes later I hear a loud bang. I rush back into the living-room and see that the TV screen is cracked. It looks like she threw the remote control at the TV.

'What the hell did you do that for? You could've hurt Harry,' I shout at her.

'Barney's voice pisses me off,' came the reply.

I shake my head and clean up the glass.

'I'm seriously worried about you. I'm taking tomorrow off and we're going to the doctors together.'

Laura looks at me with the saddest expression but says nothing.

CHAPTER FOURTEEN

At ten o'clock the following morning my mobile rings; it's Laura.

'David, I'm outside, can I come in?'

I let my ex-wife into my house. 'You've got a key, you don't need my permission.'

'Where's Harry?' She asks.

'In his bedroom watching Thomas of course. Shall I call him down?'

'Not yet, I want to have a chat first.'

'You're worrying me; what's up?'

'We've been house hunting in Ireland the past week and found a house in Limerick that Sean's desperate to buy.'

'Sounds good to me.'

'He doesn't just want it as a holiday home, he wants to retire there.'

'Oh, I see.'

'The house and the surrounding area are amazing. I just don't know what to do.'

'Because of Harry?'

'Yep.'

'I've heard him talking about this before, so it couldn't have been a surprise,' I say.

'I know, but I just thought that it was a pipe dream. I really didn't think it would actually happen. Sean's been looking at houses on the internet for ages. He went over there about a month ago to view a few of them and really liked this one house. I went with him and just loved it. It's perfect.'

'He must know your reservations.'

'Yes we've talked about it at length, but he keeps on saying that we'll only be a sixty minute flight away, but it's not as simple as that, is it?'

'No of course not. Laura, I totally understand your dilemma and I really do sympathise, but I can't advise you either way, I'm afraid it's totally your call.'

'I know, I know...'

Living circumstances seems a hot topic right now.

'You seem stressed, what's up?' She asks.

'Kerry's spending all her time in Brighton. I just can't see a solution to this.'

'That's easy, just go along to one of the Streatham bus stops, there's always women waiting there. Just take one of them home,' Harry replies.

I didn't notice that he was standing in the hallway apparently listening to our conversation.

'And how are you, Harry?' Laura asks, giving her son a hug.

'Lee Mack still hasn't replied to me.'

Laura looks at me but I shake my head. She's picks up the signal not to pursue the Lee Mack dialogue.

'How did it go with the priest yesterday?' She asks her son.

'He said that the wedding's going to be an hour. I told him he's taking the piss.'

'And what did he say?'

'He just laughed. Anyway, we're leaving after ten minutes. We want to get back to the reception before all the crowds eat the pork pies.'

'You're both staying for the whole of the wedding, OK? It'll be the best moment of your life,' an emotional Laura replies.

'No, it'll be the worst moment of my life if I get to the reception too late.'

'Is Bernadette excited about the wedding?' Laura asks Harry.

'She doesn't want to walk down that church gangway like they do in the films, she wants to run down it cos she doesn't want to waste everyone's time.'

Laura's tense expression visibly softens in reaction to Harry's comment. She's understandably concerned about the prospect of a move to Ireland and I'm guessing that's a decision that has to be made sooner rather than later. I know that financially they're reasonably well off, but can they afford to keep two houses? If not, could she go to Ireland but still pop across the Irish Sea on a regular basis? Conversely, if Sean really knows the torment that she's going through would he still go ahead with it, especially given her mental health history? I would never want Laura to go through that ever again.

CHAPTER FIFTEEN: 1994

It took a lot of persuasion to convince Laura that she needs to see a doctor. She kept telling me that she's just worn out with the physical effort in looking after Harry and that's all. Whether she believes that herself I'm not sure, but I certainly don't.

'On average how many hours sleep do you get every night?' The doctor asks Laura.

'Two to three hours.'

'You really need seven or eight hours.'

'I am aware of that but my son doesn't seem to need much sleep and when he's up we have to be as well.'

'Why doesn't he require more sleep?'

'No fucking idea. You tell me.'

'He's got a lot of behavioural issues. We're seeing a psychiatrist and she thinks he's got ODD and OCD, but to be honest that's just scratching the surface,' I add.

'Laura, the lack of sleep and the constant worrying about Harry is obviously affecting your physical and mental well-being. I can give you something that will help calm your nerves and something to help you sleep?'

'Yes please; I'd take anything right now.'

'And what about you, David? How are you coping?'

'OK I suppose, but I'm worried about Laura and Harry. We're all feeling the strain.'

'I can also give you some medication?'

'No thanks. For the time being the priority is Laura.' I tell the doctor.

'But I need to be up for Harry,' Laura informs me.

'For the next few weeks I'm going to be doing that. We need you to get as much rest as possible in order for you to make a full recovery,' I say.

'David's right. Although it'll put extra pressure on him you're the one who really needs to take it easy right now. I can't emphasise that enough. You can't go on the way you are now,' the doctor tells Laura.

'You're beginning to scare me.'

'No, you shouldn't be scared, you just need to follow what David and I are telling you, that's all.'

Laura nods. We leave shortly afterwards. I'm feeling better that we've got a couple of prescriptions for Laura but she now looks more worried than when she came in.

CHAPTER SIXTEEN

'So what sort of a week did you have?' I ask my son.

'Whenever I tell the staff workers that I want to go to London to see the McDonalds in Piccadilly Circus they always tell me that one of them have to come with me. Are they spies?'

'No they're not spies. Although you're allowed to walk around Croydon on your own or with Bernadette, if you go too much further, like London, then someone has to accompany you. It's for your own safety.'

'But I know what train to catch. Bernadette and me want to sing all the *My Little Pony* songs on the train to cheer up all the other passengers. I can't do that if a house spy is watching me.'

'That's the reason why someone has to be with you. Remember what happened when you left the train without me and wandered around London on your own? You started to talk to yourself and those thugs picked up on that and mugged you? I don't want that to happen again. You have to be careful.'

'But I'm big and strong now. Anyway Bernadette will kick the shit out of them so I can just watch her do that.'

The age of chivalry is not dead yet, certainly not in Croydon.

'Why do you think I'm going with you on your honeymoon?'

'Because you love Halifax of course.'

'No, it's to protect you. Anyway, tonight your mum, Sean, Kerry, Niall, Bernadette, Alice, Robert and Stephanie are all coming to us for dinner.'

'Didn't that Brighton chick say that you were a boring arsehole? So why is she coming?'

'Kerry never said that about me.'

Harry has an amazing memory for events that happened years ago, so I'm half expecting him to give me a date and time when my wife called me a boring arsehole.

'I just thought that was the reason why she's staying in Brighton.'

'No, it isn't,' I reply, a little relieved.

'Anyway that's way too many people in the house, I'm going to keep bumping into everyone and it's going to hurt my shoulders. Can't you get rid of a few of them?'

'No, they're all coming.'

'What's for dinner?'

'I'm going to order some pizza and make a salad.'

'You're not going to have lettuce in the salad are you?'

'Yes I am.'

'But I don't like the green colour in the lettuce. It's too light. Can you make the lettuce a darker green?'

'No, I'm afraid I can't. You don't have to eat it. The others like lettuce, especially when it's the lighter green colour.'

'Well they must be a bit mad in the head.'

I thought that as the wedding is only two weeks away it would be a good idea to get everyone together now as opposed to next weekend. I contacted Kerry a couple of days ago and fully expected her to decline, but was pleasantly surprised when she agreed to it. Could this be the turning point?

Two hours later all the guests are tucking into their pizza and the drinks are flowing.

Robert is an ex class friend of Harry and his mother is Stephanie. To say that Stephanie is sexually active would be an understatement, even though she's now in her fifties. I rarely saw her with the same man more than once before she married Ray a couple of years ago.

'Where's Ray?' I ask Stephanie.

'Fuck knows, we're separated.'

'I'm sorry to hear that. What happened, if you don't mind me asking?'

'He's a boring prick. He was always more interested in *Pointless* and *The Chase* than anything I could offer him.'

'Does he still live with you?'

'No, he left a couple of months ago.'

'I have to say I'm surprised. He seemed like a nice guy.'

'Yeah, he wouldn't hurt a fly, actually he was about as interesting as a fly. Anyway, David, I apologise for dashing off early but I'm meeting someone shortly. He's fourteen years younger than me, so I'm hopeful of a good night. Robert can make his own way back.'

With that she kisses me on my cheek, says her goodbyes to everyone and leaves. I think the only way she would have stayed longer if I had invited the Chippendales to the party.

Robert approaches me.

'What soft drinks do you have?' he asks.

'Well, we have Coke, lemonade and orange juice.'

'Shit, shit and shit,' came the reply.

'OK, so what drink would you like?'

'Water.'

Does water classify as a soft drink?

'I've got plenty of water. I'll get a bottle from the fridge.'

'No bottled water. That tastes like mud.'

'OK, I'll get you a glass of tap water.'

'I fucking hate glasses. I'm afraid of dropping them.'

'OK, so where do we go from here?'

'I only drink water directly from the tap.'

I show Robert the kitchen and he sticks his head under the tap for a couple of minutes.

'That water's diluted, you should've told me,' Robert says as he walks into the living-room with water covering most of his face and hair. He doesn't seem to notice.

Laura and Sean walk over to me.

'A wonderful gathering, David. We're so excited about the wedding,' Sean tells me.

'Yeah, it's going to be an amazing day. The nerves are creeping up on me a bit though.'

'Tell me about it. I haven't slept well for a while now,' Laura adds.

'What's happening with the house move?' I bravely ask.

'All I have to do is persuade Laura. I keep telling her that Limerick isn't a million miles away from Streatham, but she's not convinced. The estate agents have rung me several times saying that another family are interested and I have to make my mind up pretty soon or I might lose it. What do you think, David?'

'Leave me out of it, it's your decision,' I reply, holding my hands up.

'That's another reason why I can't sleep at night,' Laura says.

'It's such a beautiful house at a good price and the area is lovely and peaceful. I know you'll be happy there,' Sean tells his wife.

'I won't be at peace if I'm away from Harry,' Laura quickly replies.

Laura and Sean look defiantly at each other, but don't say anything. I feel as if I'm intruding into a private conversation, so I make my excuses and approach Harry and Bernadette.

Although I didn't give my opinion I wouldn't want Laura to live permanently in Ireland. When Harry was really young Laura simply couldn't cope with his behaviour and it got to the point where Harry and I had to move out. She has been living with that guilt ever since.

'So what do you want to do tomorrow?' I ask Harry.

'Let's visit twelve car parks,' came the reply.

'You're a genius, Harry. That's an amazing suggestion. Boy am I glad we're getting married,' Bernadette adds.

'Sorry, I'm a little confused?'

'What do you mean?' Harry asks.

'Why are we going to car parks?'

Harry and Bernadette both look at me with exasperated expressions.

'Are you transforming into a Streatham simpleton?'

'Don't be so rude.'

'Well what is it you don't understand?'

'You said you wanted to visit car parks, so what do you want to do in the car parks?' I ask.

'We'll go to twelve car parks - in Streatham, Thornton Heath, Norbury, Brixton, Stockwell and Vauxhall. We'll stay in each car park for twenty minutes and we'll note all the cars that arrive after us and when I get home I'll copy it all to an Excel spreadsheet.'

'What information are you going to write down?'

'The make of the car, its colour, number plate, arrival time, the car park rating and how much petrol they've got left.'

'And what are you going to do with all this information?'

'Just study it.'

'But if you spend twenty minutes in each car park that's going to take four hours, plus all the travelling time between all the locations.'

'If you can't be arsed to come along we'll hitchhike to all the car parks. It's easy.'

'That isn't happening. How many times have I warned you about talking to strangers, let alone get in their cars?'

'But they'll love it when we'll narrate some of the Thomas episodes.'

I find it so disturbing that even at thirty years of age Harry still hasn't got the concept of the dangers of engaging with strangers. I have warned him so many times about this, but all to no avail.

I leave Harry and Bernadette to work out their car park strategy and head towards Kerry and Niall.

'Thanks again for coming along, it's great to see you both,' I say to my wife and her son.

Niall takes my hand and walks me towards the fridge. He guides my hand to open the fridge door and then takes my index finger to point at a can of Coke.

'Kerry, can he have a Coke?' I ask.

'Yeah, if you don't give it to him he might kick off. I really don't want that right now.'

I hand over the can. He rests it against his cheek and then his knee before opening it.

'Tomorrow morning I've got to take Harry and Bernadette to various car parks; sorry about that.'

'How long will that take?' Kerry replies.

'I'm afraid the best part of five hours.'

'We came all the way up here to see you and now you'll be gone most of tomorrow. How come you didn't tell me?'

'I only just found out. Kerry, it's one of the last weekends when I'll be able to spend some time with him. After the wedding it's all going to change.'

'I really don't see how much difference there'll be before or after the wedding. We made a special effort, can't you put him off?'

'No I can't.'

'Well in that case we might as well leave now. I'll say my goodbyes and make up some excuse why we have to go. Don't worry, I won't embarrass you.'

'I think you're overreacting.'

'You keep telling me that I don't spend any time with you but when I free up my weekend you bugger off at the first opportunity.'

'This just came up. I didn't plan it that way.'

Kerry doesn't respond and spends the next ten minutes mingling with the other guests and then leaves without acknowledging me.

CHAPTER SEVENTEEN: 1994

'How has Harry been in the past week?' Carol asks.

'Same as the week before and the week before that and, in fact, the last three years. No change,' Laura replies.

'I understand you're taking medication for your nerves and for sleeping. Has that helped?'

'Yes, a bit, especially for sleeping, but it's making me very lethargic and spaced out. Not a nice feeling.'

'Maybe it's just a case of getting used to the medication. It's early days.'

I think Carol was expecting a response but Laura just stares at the wall for no obvious reason. There's no photographs or framed certificates, just plain dull wallpaper.

'Is he still hitting you with the same intensity?' Carol asks us.

I hand over the paper with all the latest stats.

'Yeah, looks pretty much the same. So just to summarise where we are. Harry's attacking you both about eight or nine times daily. That includes mainly pinching and kicking. Is that right?'

'Yes,' I reply.

'And I presume the sleeping is still erratic?'

'Yeah, he still only sleeps two to three hours a night,' I respond.

I look at Laura and she's still staring at the wall, almost in a trance.

'And you're up with him now?' She asks me.

'Yes, Laura needs her sleep more than me at the moment.'

'What do you do for a living?'

'I'm a postman.'

'So it's quite physical. How are you coping at the moment without much sleep?'

'It's hard, but needs must.'

'OK, so I still think Harry has ODD and OCD. I also think he may have ADHD,' Carol tells us.

'And what's that?' Laura asks.

I didn't even think that she was listening.

'Attention deficit hyperactivity disorder. It's a behavioural disorder that includes symptoms such as inattentiveness, hyperactivity and impulsiveness. It's also associated with anxiety and sleep disorders. Harry seems to fall into these categories.'

'You've thrown all these labels at us but you've said nothing constructive so far to help us improve our dire situation with our son,' Laura replies.

'Harry's a complicated child. It's not a short fix solution, it's going to take a lot of sessions to get the whole picture. You just have to be patient with me on this.'

Laura shakes her head but doesn't respond. She then continues to stare blankly at the wall behind Carol.

'How often does Harry look at you when he speaks?'

'It's only when we get right in his face and point at his eyes and say 'looking'. We then have to physically direct his face towards us and even then he just glances at us for a second or two. Do you know why he doesn't make any eye contact?' I ask.

'I've got a few ideas but I want to find out more about Harry before I can come to any sort of conclusions.'

'Now you're worrying me. You were quick to diagnose him with ODD, OCD and ADHD so why are you now holding back?'

It's nothing sinister. As I said I need more information. Now let's go through an average Harry day.'

We spend the next thirty minutes discussing my son. Carol didn't offer any more opinions, she just took notes and asked questions, all of which I answered. Laura didn't say another word and the journey home was spent in silence.

Although I find it heart-breaking to hear all the medical labels that Harry seems to have accumulated recently I suppose it can only help him in the long term. I just have to face up to this new reality. However, Laura doesn't seem to be taking any of this on board.

'Why are you so dismissive of everything Carol says?' I ask her.

'She talks through her arse.'

'How can you say that? You picked up on Harry's slow development way before me which prompted us seeing Carol, didn't you? I'm just confused by your sudden negative attitude to all of this. Surely she can only help us?'

'She hasn't even met Harry and doesn't show any interest in doing so. What does that tell you?'

I agree with that last point and I'll bring it up with Carol at the next meeting but it still doesn't hide the fact that Laura has lost interest in this whole process and that worries me.

CHAPTER EIGHTEEN

It's nine thirty-two in the morning as I park my car at a half full Streatham car park. It's the beginning of what promises to be a long and somewhat tedious day. That's my take anyway, but looking at the excitement on the faces of Harry and Bernadette they seem to have a totally different outlook.

I pay the meter and return to Harry and Bernadette. They are standing by the entrance with pen and paper at the ready.

'So what now?' I ask.

'Cheer up old man, this is going to be the best day of your life,' Harry tells me.

I somehow doubt that. I'm not in a positive frame of mind today. My bust up with Kerry yesterday has made me more depressed than ever about our future together. Although she tried to keep her exit as discreet as possible, nearly everyone noticed that something was wrong and quizzed me directly after her departure. I tried to play it down by saying that she wanted to get back to Brighton for Niall's sake, to his own routine, but I think they all saw through my lies.

The first car pulls into the car park and Harry waves at him to stop.

'What's the problem?' The driver asks.

'How much petrol have you got left?' Harry asks.

'What's it got to do with you?'

'I need to know for my Excel spreadsheet.'

'I don't know what you're talking about.'

'How much did your hair piece cost?' Harry inquires.

'Excuse me, my son's autistic and he's just carrying out a personal survey about all the different cars coming into this car park. I'm sorry for the confusion,' I tell the driver.

My explanation doesn't cut any ice as he just drives on.

'It's OK, Bernadette, he has three quarters of a tank left. I noticed it when he was adjusting his hair piece,' Harry tells his wife-to-be.

'Harry, that man doesn't have a hair piece,' I say.

'Of course he has. Anyway, how the hell would you know? You haven't got any hair left.'

'I've noted the car was a Land Rover Discovery Sports Diesel SW, the colour was red and the registration number was LA67 RSF,' Bernadette tells Harry.

'That's excellent work. Look out, there's another car coming,' Harry says.

I was right, it's going to be a very long day.

Two hours later a car pulls into the Brixton car park and as usual Harry and Bernadette signal for the driver to stop.

'What do you think of this car park?' Harry asks the driver

'Just amazing. It lets me park my car,' the driver rather sarcastically replies.

'Good answer. I'll give that an eight out of ten,' Harry replies as he jots down the answer.

'Why the hell are you playing Ed Sheeran?' Bernadette inquires.

'It's just a song on the radio.'

'His ginger hair disgusts me,' she replies.

'And he never combs it,' Harry chips in.

The driver now looks totally baffled.

'Anyway we've got all your details so you can park your car now. There's only one spot available over there,' Harry tells him, but another driver overtakes him and parks his car.

Heated words are exchanged between the two drivers but Harry doesn't even notice.

'Shall we move onto the next car park? It'll leave a space for that guy,' I say as the frustrated driver is staring across at us.

'Nah, serves him right for listening to ginger haired singers.'

At eight minutes past four we're finally making our way back home. Harry has just informed me that they stopped 151 cars. He wasn't able to obtain the petrol consumption in only six cars but he told me he wasn't bothered as he'll work out an average for the other one hundred and forty-five cars and apply it to the missing six. I'm still not sure what they are going to do with all this information but at this point I just don't care. I just want to go home and crack open a can of beer.

We passed several supermarkets during our car park adventure and to save some time I asked Harry if we could stop at the supermarket car parks but he told me that 'they're not proper car parks, just wannabe car parks.' Fair enough.

'What was your favourite part of the day?' Harry asks me as we're approaching Bernadette's house.

'Seeing the both of you together.'

'What do you mean?'

'It was just lovely seeing you both enjoying yourselves and being in each other's company.'

'We were just doing our job, Mister McCarthy,' Bernadette replies.

'You mean collecting all the information about the cars?' I ask.

'No, just practicing for our husband and wife jobs that we're going to get soon. We're excited about our new jobs.'

I smile in reply but it's one of the most uncomplicated and honest statements about a relationship that I've ever heard. I wish I could walk away and compose myself but that's not practical as I'm driving. I must tell Alice, she'll just love that and so will Laura.

When we arrive at Bernadette's house Alice invites us in. To be honest I'm absolutely exhausted as I've been standing in car parks all day. Harry and Bernadette are not too clued up on road safety so I had to be alongside them all day just in case.

'How did it go today?' Alice asks as she hands me a beer.

'Twelve car parks and 151 cars, it was exhausting, but it was just wonderful to see them together,' I reply.

I then told Alice about Bernadette's married job remark earlier. She looked down at the floor after I mentioned it and it took a couple of minutes before she could carry on with our conversation.

I've been through so many negative encounters and situations with my son – whether it's the teachers at his nursery school, professionals who kept telling me that Harry is not capable of doing this or that, his own peers mocking him etc, etc, so whenever anything positive happens to him it's magnified many times over, so I completely understand Alice's reaction.

'How do you feel about Harry and Bernadette sharing a bed together?' Alice asks me.

'A little apprehensive if I'm honest. Although I've done the sex talk with him so many times I still don't think he's grasped it.'

'I feel the same way about Bernadette. I know that they've spent time in each other's bedrooms, but they've never slept together.'

'I don't really know how sexually motivated Harry is. He certainly notices females and sometimes makes inappropriate comments directly to them, but I really don't think that he's interested beyond that. He's never made any sexual remarks about Bernadette.'

'I'll have another chat with Bernadette. It's probably best that we do this separately.'

'Of course. My parents never went through that talk with me. I just picked it up at school. What about you?' I ask.

'I can clearly remember mum trying to tell me everything. I was confused and embarrassed. The conversation lasted only a few minutes. I spent the next year trying to fill in the gaps.'

Harry and Bernadette burst into the living-room.

'We're going to see Lee Mack tomorrow,' Harry says.

'What do you mean?'

'He's playing a warm up show at the Leicester Square theatre at four o'clock and another one at seven o'clock.'

'Are tickets still available?'

'Yeah, I checked. People don't want to see him since he's had that beard. I want to get him to sign my *Not*

Going Out and my *Thomas And The Magic Railroad* DVD covers.'

'Harry, the chances of meeting him are slim, so don't get too excited.'

'We'll get to meet him. He arrives at the theatre at three.'

'How do you know that?'

'It's on the Lee Mack Is Very Funny website.'

Trust Harry to find such a website.

'I think he's a load of old shit but I want to go and hold onto those DVD covers because Harry's hands can get a bit sweaty,' Bernadette tells us.

'David, Greg's got a really important business lunch tomorrow afternoon which involves the partners. I'm afraid I can't get out of it. I'm really sorry,' Alice says.

'Not a problem. I'll ask Laura. I think she'll be delighted to come along. OK, let's book those tickets.'

When I arrived home I contacted Laura. She was thrilled at the prospect of spending an evening with us all. It's been so long since I've had a night out with her; I'm looking forward to it.

CHAPTER NINETEEN: 1994

'Do we really have to see that psychiatrist again? She's fucking no use whatsoever,' Laura tells me.

'Yes, we'll continue with the sessions. We're making progress, just try to stick with it,' I reply.

'The only practical advice she's given us so far has been that stupid Sunday box idea. What was all that about?'

'Laura, it's all trial and error. OK, that didn't work out for us but the fact that it didn't must have helped her in some way.'

'Don't tell me you're buying into all her claptrap?'

'What have we got to lose? We both agreed that seeing a psychiatrist was the first step in looking into Harry's problems, didn't we?'

Laura doesn't respond.

'Are you just pissed off that you're missing the Barney episodes on our cracked television?'

'Barney certainly makes more sense than Carol, that I have no doubt,' Laura finally replies.

'Why don't you take your sleeping tablet and get ready for bed. You'll feel better about it all in the morning.' I say, although I don't believe she will.

I watch her swallow her tablet and climb the stairs to the bedroom. She doesn't say goodnight to me or her son.

I give Harry his bath and put him in his bed. I crack open a can of Castlemaine and after taking a couple of sips Harry comes down to the living-room and puts on *The Mask* video. At least it's a film that I can watch, but lately I've been falling to sleep shortly after the nightly video starts, which isn't ideal as when I wake up there's always an assortment of sweet packets on the floor, which is usually accompanied by an empty can of Coke or lemonade.

Tonight though, Laura's erratic behaviour dominates my thoughts. With the new medication she seems listless, but yet she has moments of extreme anger and bitterness.

It's like living with a different person.

CHAPTER TWENTY

Thirteen days to go before Harry gets married. As it's getting nearer I'm getting increasingly nervous. Is it because I just want everything to go well on the day? Am I worried about how Harry and Bernadette will cope with married life? Or am I just feeling downcast because I'll be seeing a lot less of Harry afterwards? It's probably a combination of all three.

'Can I have Frosties this morning?' Harry asks as he enters the kitchen.

'Yeah no problem.'

'But don't put any milk on them.'

'Harry, I've been making your breakfast for nearly thirty years and I've never once put milk on your Frosties.'

'I didn't know if you forgot. You're getting a bit decrepit now.'

Will I miss these early morning chats? Of course I will.

'What crazed lunatic puts milk on their Frosties? It makes them soggy and ugly. I don't like eating damp food.'

'Orange juice?'

'Piss off. Last week some of the orange bits got stuck in my teeth and I had a nightmare about it. That's it – no more orange juice for the rest of my life.'

No sitting on the fence with Harry.

'Did you enjoy seeing everyone yesterday?' I ask.

'They were all laughing too much and I could see all their teeth. I didn't like that.'

'You don't laugh much do you, Harry?'

'No definitely not. It wastes my time.'

'Do you miss work?' I inquire.

'No because all the customers are bastards. Where's the baked beans? Where's the milk? Where's the bread? Where's the beer?'

'OK, Harry, I get the idea. I hope you don't call them bastards.'

'Sometimes I call them fuckwits if they're disturbing me when I'm trying to put out the butter and I'm in a bad mood cos my hands are frozen.'

'You should never call the customers fuckwits, that's going to get you into trouble.'

'What about little shits?'

'No, don't ever call them rude names, OK?'

'They deserve it.'

'And what do they say when you tell them they're fuckwits?' I nervously ask.

'They always look angry and then they notice my lanyard and smile at me.'

Harry has been working for the supermarket *PriceLess* for the past fourteen years. Despite his protests he seems to enjoy his job. He wears a lanyard to identify that he's special needs and he's therefore fully entitled to call the customers fuckwits. He only works on Saturdays and has been granted a month off special leave in preparation for his wedding.

'Do you want to go in and say hello to your friends at *PriceLess* today?'

'Nah, it's different staff on Sundays and most of the men all have grey hair. I don't like grey hair, it looks silly. I don't want to go anywhere near those grey guys.'

Sometimes when I go for a coffee with Harry, Kerry and Niall on a Friday, Harry pops into *PriceLess* for an hour and helps them stack the shelves – unpaid voluntary work.

'Do you know what the best job in the world is?' Harry asks.

'No, I don't.'

'It's the person who makes the plastic bit at the end of the shoe laces. Whoever does that must be a genius. Without that plastic bit you wouldn't be able to fit the shoe laces through the holes in the shoes and then the shoes will be loose without any shoelaces and they'll fall off onto the pavement when you're walking and you'd have to go around Streatham wearing just your socks.'

Good point.

'Does that leprechaun bloke come from Cork in Ireland?' Harry inquires.

'Are you talking about Sean?'

'It's the bloke who lives with my mum and he has brown carpet on his stairs.'

'Yes that's Sean, but he's from Limerick. Why do you ask?'

'Because he speaks like his arse is on fire.'

There's no answer to that.

'When we went to that Cork place on Monday the eighteenth of August 2003 there were only two suitcase carousels at the airport; that's amazing.'

'It's a small airport.'

'Why?'

'It's not a big city.'

'Is it because nobody understands what the hell Cork people are banging on about and just don't bother visiting because there's no point.'

'Cork is one of the most beautiful cities in the world and your grandparents are from there so you should be proud of your roots.'

'The suitcase carousel waiting time at Gatwick airport is the worst in England, it's thirty-three minutes and twenty-one seconds. When we were at Cork airport we waited thirteen minutes and eighteen seconds, so maybe people are fed up of waiting in London and decide to go to Cork instead?'

'OK, Harry, I think we've exhausted this conversation.'

A conversation that consisted of talking about damp Frosties, being informed that I was now decrepit, orange bits in teeth causing nightmares, Harry not laughing as it wastes his time, calling customers fuckwits, disliking men with grey hair, plastic bits at the end of shoe laces and the baggage carousel situation at Cork Airport. Question Time doesn't even cover such diverse subjects.

'I'm going on YouTube to looks at videos of the suitcase carousel at Cork airport,' Harrys says as he dashes off.

My thoughts again turn to Kerry. I haven't spoken to her since she abruptly left the party on Friday. To some extent I do understand her frustration concerning the car park activity but she must also realise that my time with Harry right now is very precious and I just couldn't waste that opportunity to spend that time with him and Bernadette.

I pick up the phone and dial her number; she answers straight away.

'How's it going?' I ask.

'OK.'

'Look I'm sorry about Friday. I hadn't planned to spend most of Saturday at car parks but that's what Harry wanted to do.'

'Maybe I overreacted. I was just looking forward to spending some time together but for one reason or another that doesn't seem to be happening much these days.'

'Is it alright if I pop down to yours next weekend?'

'We'll see. I'll let you know.'

The conversation carries on for a few more minutes but it's strained and I'm relieved when we terminate it. I'm not sure why she didn't agree to meeting up next weekend. It's obvious she hasn't got anything already planned as she would have said so.

By midday Laura arrives. We pick up Bernadette and make our way to the Underground.

'We've got to get the Victoria line from Brixton to Green Park, this takes nine minutes. We then have to walk to the Piccadilly line. This takes five and a half minutes for me and Bernadette, but probably twelve minutes for you. Then we go from Green Park to Leicester Square. This journey just stops at Piccadilly Circus and takes only three minutes. When we get out of Leicester Square tube the theatre is only a four minute walk for me and Bernadette but for you it'll take…'

'OK, Harry, thanks for that comprehensive journey itinerary,' I tell my son.

'It's only one o'clock. The show doesn't start until four. Why are we going so early?' Laura asks me.

'Harry wants to meet Lee Mack beforehand at the stage door.'

'And how long do we have to wait for that?'

'Harry found out that he gets to the theatre at around three but he wants to be there by two at the latest.'

'In that case do you mind if I go shopping in Oxford Street and meet you later?'

'You're going to be missing out on the opportunity of a life time. You're aware of that I presume?'

'I don't even like him. I'm doing this to spend time with Harry.'

That's fifty percent of our contingent who are going to see Lee Mack but don't actually like him. I'm sure that Lee will change their minds by the end of his performance.

'Any more news on the house front?' I ask.

'None. I feel bad for Sean because he's set his heart on getting it and it would be a lovely place to retire, there's no doubt in my mind about that, but I'm torn and just don't know what to do.'

'Well for the next few hours try not to think about it and just enjoy the afternoon.'

Laura smiles at me but it's a forced smile. She looks worn out. Even though we've been divorced for twenty years I care deeply about her and I'm really concerned for her health.

Harry's journey timings are pretty accurate, so at ten minutes to two Harry, Bernadette and myself are waiting at the stage door.

'Why do you like Lee Mack?' I ask Harry.

'When he's saying funny things he always looks a bit pissed off.'

'And why don't you like him, Bernadette?'

'Only Lenny Henry and Harry are funny; nobody else.'

'Have you tried on your wedding dress?'

'Yeah, it's white and too long. I look like a ghost.'

'I'm sure you'll look beautiful.'

'Are you going to the wedding?' She asks.

'Of course I am. I can't wait.'

'But they're showing the Arsenal - Liverpool game on Sky at the same time. I thought you were an Arsenal fan?'

'I am, but I'll give the game a miss on that day.'

'Did you hear that, Harry, your dad's not watching the Arsenal game?'

'Yeah I know. He always watches Arsenal when they're on the telly. I really don't know why he arranged the wedding at exactly the same time as the game. What was he thinking?'

The conversation continues in this vain for the next seventy-five minutes or so and at seven minutes past three (I've been hanging around Harry too long) Lee Mack arrives at the stage door.

'What fucking time do you call this?' Harry asks, as he points to his watch.

'I'm sorry, what do you mean?'

'You were supposed to be here at three. What the hell happened?'

'I'm sorry. My son's autistic. He saw on one website that you arrive at three,' I say.

His tense expression visibly relaxes.

'Anyway, why the fuck are you still wearing that stupid beard? I don't want to go to the show now cos you're going to be absolutely shit.'

Understandably he looks confused.

'Anyway can you sign my *Thomas The Tank Engine* DVDs?'

'Harry, forget about the Thomas DVDs. Lee wasn't in any of them.'

Harry tuts but hands over the *Not Going Out* DVDs, which Lee signs.

'Have you got any BICs razors with you?' Harry asks.

'No, I haven't.'

'There's a Boots chemist around the corner, you can definitely get them in there.'

'Harry's a bit obsessed about beards,' I explain.

Lee smiles but still looks perplexed.

'And you can forget about being my best man.'

Lee is now totally baffled. I don't bother to explain.

I ask Lee if he'll pose for a photo with Harry and he kindly agrees. Lee was smiling in the photo but Harry was looking angrily at him or more specifically his beard.

Lee shook Harry's hand and seemed relieved to be entering the safe confines of the theatre.

'He was such a nice guy, wasn't he?' I say to Harry.

'He's fucked up my afternoon. What are we going to do now?'

'What do you mean?'

'I'm not going to the show.'

'Don't tell me it's because of the beard?'

'Of course it is.'

'I've spent over a hundred pounds on these tickets. We're definitely going.'

'Just get more money out of the bank, they've got loads.'

With that Bernadette and Harry walk away. I hear Bernadette telling Harry to hand over the DVD covers because of his 'clammy hands'.

I contact Laura and explain the change of plans. Soon after we all end up in KFC.

'The Americans are the best cooks in the world. They invented KFC, McDonalds and Burger King. How come England doesn't have any good cooks?' A more relaxed Harry announces.

'We have plenty, what about Gordon Ramsay?'

'I love it when he tells the customers to fuck off but his food is shit.'

'I disagree. The best meal I ever had was when he was in charge of Claridge's. It was amazing.'

'Did you have steak and kidney pie with chips?'

'No, I had lots of different dishes. The best one was venison.'

'Sounds rubbish. What the hell is it?'

'It's deer.'

'You fucking ate Bambi, are you crazy?'

'Are you now going to be in the remake of the Bambi film?' Bernadette asks.

A simple food discussion ends in being accused of killing one of Disney's most beloved creations.

Harry and Bernadette stare at me as if I'm the devil incarnate, but when the KFC bargain bucket arrives they soon forget about my homicidal background.

'I really didn't know that you were a murderer. If I did I would've thought twice about marrying you,' a smiley Laura remarks.

'It happened after we broke up.'

'Was that your way of coping with it?'

'Well it was an extremely stressful time. In fact it was the worst time of my life,' I say, suddenly remembering the pain of our break up. How can a light hearted moment turn serious so quickly?

Laura's smile disappears. 'I'm sorry, I didn't mean to…'

'No need to apologise. Who would've thought that after all these years it still gets to me? I've been feeling pretty emotional lately. I've got a lot on my mind,' I say.

'Of course.'

'I'm being stupid. It was a million years ago.'

'Let's not forget that we had some great years together, didn't we?' Laura says.

'Yeah, we did. Remember when Harry was about six and we took him to see that pantomime? What was it again?'

'Cinderella.'

'That's it and when there was a quiet moment during the performance and he shouted at the actors…'

'You're all a bunch of bastards,' Laura smiles.

'I was mortified. As we were only a few rows from the front, a few of the actors actually looked over to see who gave them that critique.'

'We told him off but after he went to bed that night we couldn't stop laughing.'

'Yes we did, didn't we?'

Laura grins at me. It's the same expression that I recollect from many years ago.

'I've been thinking about the past a lot lately, some memories are so painful but I'm also remembering the good times as well, which is nice because for a long time I could only recall our last couple of years together,' I say.

'Yes, I still think about the end of our marriage. I just remember those psychiatrist sessions. I was in such a bad way and we just didn't know what the hell was going on with Harry.'

'Yeah, I know but look at him now.'

We both glance at Harry and Bernadette.

'Only three hundred and eight hours and twenty-one minutes before we go back to that crumbling religious building. You'll be wearing your ghost outfit and I'll have to wear a tie that will probably strangle me. Afterwards we'll have those pork pies with the salt and vinegar crisps,' Harry says.

'Wow, I'm really looking forward to that meal,' Bernadette replies.

CHAPTER TWENTY-ONE: 1994

'Fat woman,' Harry shouts as he points to a lady ahead of us in the Post Office queue.

'Harry, please be quiet,' I tell my son.

'Fat, fat woman,' this time he laughs. He then breaks away from me, rushing towards the said woman and kisses her posterior. Most of the queue look on in disgust, while two teenagers start giggling. I approach the lady.

'I'm really sorry about that,' is all I can say to her.

'You obviously haven't yet taught your son any manners. I'm really insulted.'

Harry then starts laughing hysterically.

'He's totally out of control,' she shouts at me.

'Again, I can't apologise enough,' I repeat before swiftly making our exit.

'What the hell did you do that for?' I ask Harry, but he's still laughing and doesn't acknowledge me. I kneel down on the pavement to be roughly at his level. I gently twist his face so he's looking directly at me.

'You mustn't say bad things to people. They really don't like it,' I say to him, trying to keep my vocabulary as simplistic as possible.

But Harry just looks away from me.

'Do you understand what I'm saying?'

He's still not making any eye contact.

'Please speak to me,' I scream, but instead he's just staring at a fish and chip shop a few feet away from us.

I should have tried to explain to that woman that Harry is a slow developer and has other issues, which even I can't comprehend. Perhaps she would have been more sympathetic but I just wanted to get out of there as soon as possible, away from the disapproving looks that were surrounding us.

Harry is seemingly oblivious to my anxiety and the distress he caused to that lady. Despite everything I feel sorry for my boy and give him a hug. As usual he keeps his hands by his sides, he never reciprocates any sign of affection.

My greatest wish is that my son will express his feelings to me. I long for a 'normal' father and son relationship but I fear it will never happen.

I hold his hand and lead him towards the fish and chip shop.

CHAPTER TWENTY-TWO

When Laura and I dropped off Harry and Bernadette at the home they informed us that they need to redecorate their respective rooms in readiness for the next residents coming in and they also needed to do the same to their new accommodation. The consequence of this was that I had to pick Harry up this Thursday and he'll be with me until after he comes back from honeymoon. I contacted my manager, who kindly agreed that I could take special leave up to the wedding. I've been working for an IT consultancy company called *Strategy IT* for twenty years. I am a computer programmer. It can be a stressful job as there's always deadlines and I have to support various IT systems overnight. It's not exactly a bundle of laughs getting calls at two in the morning to solve some IT issue. It's a pressure that I could do without, but there is light at the end of the tunnel as I hope to retire within twelve months. Every eighteen months or so there has been a staff reorganisation at work and I've been extremely lucky to have survived them all; however I dearly wish they would make me redundant now as it'll be a lovely pay off before I retire.

I was always looking forward to retirement and spending more time with Harry, Kerry and Niall but now all those family plans are up in the air.

Even after taking the Halifax leave I still have some holidays left so I decide to take today off with the sole intention of surprising Kerry by visiting her at her school. Maybe this could kick start our relationship?

At three o'clock in the afternoon I am waiting for her outside her school gates. She teaches seven to eight-year-olds and as I'm watching the parents picking up their kids my mind goes back to when I did the same. Usually Harry was accompanied by a teacher or assistant who would tell me what Harry got up to during the course of the day. It was nearly always negative news. Even though it was such a long time ago I still feel nervous thinking about that time.

When Harry was five years old he went to a severe learning difficulties (SLD) school called Rainbow. Harry was in an autistic class throughout his time there, which was until he was eighteen.

Harry only has autistic friends and they're nearly all from Rainbow. When they get together their conversations usually involve the latest antics of *Thomas The Tank Engine*, *My Little Pony*, *Goofy*, *Lion King* etc. World politics doesn't concern them in the slightest.

Ten minutes after all the kids have gone Kerry appears. She's talking to a tall man, I'd say he's about ten years younger than her. I'm assuming he's also a teacher. They stop in the middle of the playground and continue to chat. I feel a little awkward observing her from a distance, but she looks so happy and relaxed. I haven't seen that side of her for a very long time.

Kerry notices me as she approaches the front gates. Her facial expression immediately changes.

'What are you doing here? Is everything OK?' She asks.

'Yes, sorry to startle you. I thought it'd be a nice surprise. I've taken today off.'

'Oh OK, I thought that something happened to Niall or Harry.'

On the way down here I had visions of Kerry's delightful reaction upon seeing me. She hugged and kissed me with the same passion of our early days together. Not to be.

Instead there's an awkward silence between the three of us.

'David, this is Ken. He teaches maths for the same age group as my class,' Kerry says.

I shake Ken's hand.

'I better get going. I'll see you tomorrow, Kerry. Nice to meet you, David.'

'Well aren't you pleased to see me?' I ask.

'Yes, just a little shocked. You should've told me you were coming.'

'Shall we go for something to eat?'

'I'm not hungry. I had a late lunch.'

'How about a coffee?'

'OK let's do that.'

The conversation in the coffee house is strained. I'm beginning to think that it was a mistake coming here but I'm confused why she's so quiet. It's the ideal time to chat without the obvious distractions.

'Harry was really pissed off when Lee Mack arrived late at the theatre. He said, 'what fucking time do you call this?' It's funny now but at the time…'

'Look, David, there's something I need to talk to you about.'

'What's up?' I nervously ask.

'It's just not working out is it?'

'What do you mean?'

'Our marriage. You're settled in Streatham and so am I here. I don't want to leave Brighton and you have to be near Harry. We've drifted apart the last couple of years, haven't we?'

'Kerry don't be too hasty. I'm retiring in a year, maybe I can spend the week in Brighton and then go back to Streatham at the weekends?'

'It's more complicated than that. I just don't think I love you anymore. I'm really sorry, David.'

Conversations around us suddenly stop.

This was a bombshell I did not expect and just can't believe what I'm hearing.

'Is there somebody else?'

'No. This is something I've been thinking about for the last few months. For the first time ever, Niall is settled in a home. The difference in him is amazing. I cannot do anything to jeopardise that.'

'There must be some way to save our marriage?'

'I'm afraid there isn't. It doesn't matter about the physical distance between us I just don't have the same feelings for you and I feel just awful for saying that. You've always been amazing with Niall and you're a wonderful guy. I really mean that.'

'Not wonderful enough.'

'I'm so sorry.'

'So that's it is it? A five-minute conversation to terminate our twelve year marriage?'

Kerry looks at me with tears in her eyes and simply nods.

'There's absolutely nothing I can say or do that will change your mind?'

She shakes her head.

'I'll leave you to it then.'

I get up and storm out of the coffee house. I hear her call after me but I don't look back. What's the point?

Another failed marriage under my belt.

CHAPTER TWENTY-THREE: 1994

$$\clubsuit$$

'Are you looking forward to seeing Thomas?' I ask my son as we're standing on the New Alresford platform in Hampshire. We're waiting for the *Thomas The Tank Engine* steam train, which runs on the famous Watercress line. Harry jumps up and down and looks just about as happy as I've ever seen him.

Harry has been obsessed about Thomas for the past couple of years. He has been playing the Thomas videos daily throughout this period.

I'm taking Harry on my own to give Laura a break. I'm so worried about her. She seems in another world right now and has gone from worrying sick about Harry to being totally oblivious to him. It doesn't take a rocket scientist to acknowledge that something is seriously wrong. Tomorrow I'm going to book another doctor's appointment. Laura doesn't want to see the psychiatrist as she told me that 'Carol was bonkers.' So I've re-arranged the next appointment for a couple of weeks in the hope that she will change her mind, but that's extremely doubtful.

But today is all about Harry. I tried to tell him what was happening today in the car journey here but I wasn't sure if he understood. It was only when we arrived at New Arlesford station and he saw all the Thomas posters that he twigged what was going on.

The Fat Controller is on the platform. Harry rushes over to him to give him a hug, something he's never voluntary done to Laura or me. Perhaps I should gain fifty pounds and wear a top hat and tails in order to get a hug off my son?

The look of joy on Harry's face when Thomas finally pulls into the station brings tears to my eyes. My only regret is that a healthy Laura isn't here to witness it.

Harry always looks so serious that I often wonder if he's ever feeling depressed. But today is different.

The carriage is crowded with lots of excited children. Some of them start singing songs from the Thomas videos and Harry joins in but doesn't get all the words right as he still has a limited vocabulary. However that's the first time I've ever heard him sing.

'Are you having a good time?' I ask Harry.

He doesn't reply to me but continues to smile while looking out of the train window.

We change trains twice to board James, the red train and then Henry, the green train. Along the way I buy Harry two Thomas books and three Thomas videos.

Four hours later we arrive home.

Whenever I'm out with Harry there's nearly always an incident. He sometimes hits or spits at strangers, usually kids of his own age or to Laura and myself. Only a few weeks ago I was walking across a busy street with Harry and as we were approaching the middle island he punched me in my testicles, causing me to collapse in the middle of the road. A few seconds later a car comes to a screeching halt about a foot away from me. But today it was absolutely blissful. It's no exaggeration to say that he was just about the happiest I've ever seen him. It was such an emotional day.

When we arrive home Laura is fast asleep on the couch in the living-room. A Tom and Jerry episode is on the television. Laura has been watching a lot of cartoons lately which is strange as she never did before.

I venture into the kitchen and notice that there are no dishes in the sink which indicates that Laura hasn't eaten.

Harry puts on one of his newly acquired Thomas videos and I sit on the floor to watch it with him. He attempts to play a second one but starts dozing off so I take him upstairs and lay alongside him on his bed. For once he falls asleep straight away. I intend to go downstairs to get Laura but the lack of kip in the past few weeks catches up with me and I'm soon asleep.

The end of a near perfect day.

CHAPTER TWENTY-FOUR

There is no doubt that Kerry has made her decision and will not change her mind. This was reaffirmed by a couple of texts later that evening when she let me know that she will be seeing her lawyer to start the divorce proceedings. This was something she's obviously has been planning for a while and it seems to be me that it was only a matter of time before she broke the news to me.

I know that things between us have been strained since Niall and then Kerry moved to Brighton but I honestly didn't think we were anywhere near the divorce stage.

When Kerry and Niall were living with us there were always issues, which you would expect with two autistic adults living under the same roof. Harry and Niall are at the opposite ends of the autistic spectrum but individually they contributed equally to the stress levels of the household.

Harry would often be extremely intolerant of Niall's behaviours. Sometimes he would verbally abuse Niall which usually went over Niall's head, but on occasions he would physically hurt him which was usually reciprocated. This would often lead to arguments between Kerry and me. For years Niall would physically attack me on a daily basis and Harry would constantly make cruel remarks to Kerry. He would regularly ask her when she was going to bugger off to her own flat and always suggested taking Niall with her. Kerry did not deserve that treatment but she was always extremely patient with my son and I hope that I was with Niall.

So why did it all fall apart?

Niall settling into the residential home in Brighton was a big factor. Most 'normal' children go to their local school but that doesn't usually ring true in the autistic world. A couple of Harry's friends live in a home in Rotherham because their parents couldn't find anywhere else that was appropriate to their needs in the south east area. So when there was a noticeable improvement in Niall's behaviour after a spell in his Brighton home Kerry decided to move down there to be near him. I may be doing her a disservice here but it was a decision that was made with little hesitation. She must have known at the time that our relationship would suffer because of this, but she missed her son and wanted to be with him at weekends, which I perfectly understand. The question is would I have made that same decision if the situations were reversed? I probably would.

But it changed everything.

And what timing. Ten days before Harry's wedding. If Kerry was seriously thinking of leaving me surely she could have had the decency to do it after the wedding?

My initial thoughts were not to tell anyone about our split until after the wedding but how can I explain her absence on the big day? Presumably she has no intentions of coming but to be honest I don't want her there; too much of a distraction.

The one person I won't be telling is Harry. I just can't deal with Harry's inevitable insensitive reaction.

I was up all night thinking about my conversation with Kerry. I was attempting to analyse everything she said. Why? I don't know; maybe trying to make sense of it. In the middle of the night I was convinced that she was seeing someone else. She seemed very friendly with her teacher friend Ken, but on reflection I was probably over thinking it. We have drifted apart for a while now, of that I have no doubt.

Today the reality is beginning to sink in. I've burst into tears a few times already, the first time was when I was having a shower. However, for Harry's sake I know that I've got to hold it together.

I'm going through one of the saddest days in my life right now but in a few days I hope to experience one of my happiest days ever. It's a crazy time.

I wasn't impressed with Kerry's texts last night. Barely hours after breaking up with me and she's mentioning lawyers. That was cold, ruthless and upsetting.

Last night I kept thinking how the divorce itself will pan out. There won't be any issues with the kids; she's got Niall and I have Harry. Kerry still has her flat in Streatham. She never sold it, just rented it out. The place in Brighton is rented. Maybe she'll sell the Streatham flat and buy a property in Brighton? She doesn't have many possessions in my house so hopefully that side of the divorce will be straight forward.

Will my experience from my divorce with Laura help me get through this? Only time will tell. The one similarity between the two divorces is that our autistic sons played a big part in each break up.

CHAPTER TWENTY-FIVE: 1994

'She's irritable, gets really angry at the most innocuous things and then couldn't care less over more serious matters. I've no idea what's happening,' I tell the doctor.

Laura is just sitting quietly next to me.

'Do you agree with David?' The doctor asks Laura.

'Yeah I suppose.'

'You've been taking the medicine for three weeks now, do you think it's helped?' The doctor again asks.

She looks at the floor for a couple of minutes before replying.

'Sometimes I'm calm, but mostly I feel that I can't cope with anything and just want to be left alone.'

'Doctor, the root cause is the fact that Laura couldn't handle the endless sleepless nights and more importantly Harry's erratic and aggressive behaviour. It's all got on top of her.'

'Did the psychiatrist come to any conclusion about Harry?'

'She thinks that he has OCD, ODD and ADHD but needs more sessions with us.'

'I'll leave the medicine as it is for now but come back again in a week and we'll see where we are then.'

Laura gets up and walks out of the room without saying goodbye to the doctor.

'The only benefit that I can see from the medicine is that she's sleeping at night, but it doesn't seem to have helped her moods or behaviour during the day. I'm really worried. What the hell's going on here?' I ask the doctor.

He hesitates before replying.

'I think she's heading for a nervous breakdown.'

CHAPTER TWENTY-SIX

'Don't tell me we're going to that town with the stony beach to visit that broad of yours?' Harry asks as we arrive home.

'No, we're not going there.'

'Is she coming here?'

'Nope.'

'Niall's her son, right?'

'Yes.'

'Well how come he doesn't say one word but she talks forever and ever? It makes no sense.'

'It doesn't work like that.'

'Did Niall's old man not talk then?'

'Niall's father did talk. It's just very unfortunate that Niall can't.'

'I think he's playing a game so he doesn't have to take exams or take the bins out every Friday.'

'Harry, we've been through this so many times. He's not playing a game, he just can't speak and that's it. So can we stop talking about this now?'

I don't really feel in the mood to discuss anything to do with Kerry or Niall.

'I want to have a pet,' Harry blurts out.

'Which one?'

'It's got to be a penguin. I love the way they waddle, it cracks me up. I bet the penguin will be a right laugh.'

'No, penguins need to be by the sea, they can't be kept as house pets.'

'But we can stick it in the bathtub and we'll have showers instead.'

'No, they can't spend all their time in the bathtub.'

'OK, we'll take it with us when we go to the cinema.'

'We're not getting a penguin, OK? What about another cat instead?'

'Nah, they're lazy fucks. I like eels. They're fantastic swimmers.'

'Harry, we're not having an eel as a pet. Let's forget about pets for now. As you'll be at home until the wedding, is there anything you want to do?'

'I want to go to Cork airport again. I'd love to take photos of the suitcase carousel.'

I thought if you've seen one baggage carousel you've seen them all.

'I love the way the cases go round and because there's only two carousels you can pick up the cases much quicker.'

If you can understand that logic you're a better person than me.

'So you want to go to Cork airport just to look at the baggage carousels?'

'Yes, it's so much easier to take photos because there's only two carousels and less suitcases getting in my way. That confuses me.'

It confuses me too.

The thought of going all the way to Cork just to look at baggage carousels seem ludicrous but a two or three day break in Ireland sounds exactly what I need right now.

'Do you want to ask Bernadette?'

'Of course. She loved those carousels when we went to Ireland when your mum popped her clogs.'

I ring Alice who tells me that Bernadette would love to go. She asks if I could take Bernadette as she's got a lot on for the weekend. Of course I agree. Then I have another idea, so I ring Laura.

'How are things?' I ask.

'I'm OK. Not long to go now.'

'I've got a rather strange favour to ask of you. Harry wants to go to Cork airport to take photos of the baggage carousels.'

'That's a little way out there even by Harry's standards.'

'Yeah I know, but actually I really want to go. I thought you'd like to come with us. We can be a family again for a few days. And I was thinking that we could make a trip to Limerick to look at the house. I'd like to see it and maybe offer my opinion, for what it's worth.'

'That's a wonderful idea. I'd love to look at it again without Sean pressuring me. Thanks so much for thinking of me, David.'

I feel better for doing something positive after the doom and gloom of the last twenty-four hours. The McCarthy cottage in Dunmanway, Cork, which is owned by myself and three other cousins, is available so we'll stay there.

After my divorce from Laura came through I briefly thought of moving to Ireland with Harry, but Laura would have been devastated. It's ironic that she is now seriously thinking of living in Ireland.

I'm delighted that Laura is coming with us. We haven't been on a trip like this since Harry was three, which was just before his behaviour began to have an everlasting impact on Laura and myself.

CHAPTER TWENTY-SEVEN: 1994

'I don't want you both here anymore, go find somewhere else to live,' Laura tells me.

We've just come back from the second doctor's visit in a week and after a lengthy chat with Laura he decided to refer her to Mayday hospital in Croydon for further tests. He told her that she's heading for a breakdown and needed to get into hospital as soon as possible. Although this was not unexpected it was still devastating news. Laura just scoffed at his diagnosis.

'You don't mean that,' I reply.

'Oh I do. You're both stressing me out. My life would be so much easier if you'd just fuck off.'

Harry is standing in the living-room just staring at his mother. Just how much he understands I have no idea.

'I'm not leaving you in this state. You heard what the doctor said.'

'He's a lunatic and just trying to scare me. There's no way I'm going to the hospital. I want to stay in my house without any distractions,' Laura shouts.

'Laura, you're not well, I'm not going anywhere.'

'You have to go and take him with you. He was the one who caused my illness with his endless sleepless nights, kicking and pinching me every single day and his very strange behaviour that nobody understands,' Laura bellows, pointing at Harry.

'What an awful thing to say about your son.'

'It's the truth.'

'Just take your medicine and get some sleep, you'll feel better in the morning.'

'You say that every day even though you know that's utter bullocks. I feel shit all day, every day.'

'And that's why you need to go to the hospital. They'll make you better, you've got to believe that.'

'No I don't. I've lost faith in everything.'

CHAPTER TWENTY-EIGHT

'So now Bruce Forsyth and Lee Mack are not going to be your best man have you any ideas who will be?' I ask Harry.

'I really wanted Daniel Radcliffe but he's doing a play in New York. I sent him a message on Instagram telling him that he could easily take a couple of days off and you would pay for his plane fare, but he hasn't replied yet. I don't want that other bloke in Harry Potter cos his hair is too red.'

'So Daniel Radcliffe and Rupert Grint are now out of the question. Anyone else?'

'H from Steps would be great.'

'I'm sure he would but we're running out of time, so why don't I be your best man?'

'But you're too old.'

'You were going to ask Bruce Forsyth if he wasn't dead.'

'But he was so funny and would've made a great best man's speech.'

'Harry, the weddings in nine days. Let me do it,' I plea.

'Can I have a woman? Susanna Reid would be just perfect.'

'No you can't have a woman. These celebrities don't know you, so they can't be your best man.'

'But if you go into the bank and get money out for Daniel Radcliffe's flight I'm sure he'll come.'

'Harry, I'm going to make this decision for you. I'm going to be your best man, OK?'

'But your best man's speech will be just shit. I know it will.'

'No, you're wrong. I'm going to do the most wonderful best man's speech that you've ever heard. Better than Bruce Forsyth, Lee Mack, Daniel Radcliffe, Susanna Reid and even H from Steps.'

'Oh OK, but only if you dye your hair.'

'What do you mean?'

'I know that your hair disappeared somewhere years and years ago but those little bits that didn't vanish are grey. I hate grey hair, it makes you look like one of those psychopaths. If you dye it black, like Elvis Presley's hair in 1969, you can be my best man.'

'OK, I'll dye my hair.'

I attempt to shake Harry's hand to finalise this gentleman's agreement but he just shakes his head and walks out of the kitchen. Obviously I'm a poor substitute.

The only other time I've ever had to dye my hair was twenty years ago when I applied for an IT job. The first question every job agency asked me on the phone was 'how old are you?' I was starting to go grey even back then, so I dyed my hair and I got the job. After a few weeks into the job a work colleague commented how grey I was suddenly getting. I just told him it was the stress of the job. Understandably he looked confused.

I'm probably going to look like a bit of an arsehole in the wedding photos, like those guys that I see on the commuter trains, who have a craggy face and neck, but with jet black hair. After everyone eventually finds out about my split from Kerry they'll probably think that I'm trying to look younger in order to start dating again. Nothing could be further from the truth.

However it's a small price to pay for the privilege of being Harry's best man, even though I took the unusual approach in desperately pleading with the groom to secure the role. Nevertheless, it's given me a boost. I feel very proud.

The flights to Ireland are now fully booked up for tomorrow. I'm excited to be going.

Both my parents were born in Cork and came over to England in the late fifties. Every summer holiday we had as a family was spent in Ireland, so I have a strong emotional pull to this wonderful country.

Harry has visited Ireland several times and I think he likes it there although he's always complaining about their accent. 'Why can't they speak properly?' That was another jibe he regularly aimed at Kerry. I find Irish people are on the whole extremely tolerant of my son. They are, in my opinion, such compassionate souls.

Of course Ireland reminds me of Kerry. I haven't heard from her in a couple of days and there's zero chance that I will be contacting her. What's the point? I seriously doubt that I'll see much of her in the future. I suppose I need to get a lawyer as well but that will have to wait until after the wedding and the Halifax honeymoon.

'So it's just the two of us today, what do you want to do?' I ask Harry.

'Bernadette's a lot more fun than you. Can't I spend the day with her?'

'You'll be with Bernadette for the next three days. Why not be with me today?'

I feel bad that I'm already competing with Bernadette for Harry's time.

'But all you do is watch *Emmerdale* and that black and white film about that stupid angel with grey hair. That was utter shit.'

'I think you're talking about *It's A Wonderful Life;* that's my favourite film.'

'It's a load of crap. That bit at the end when everyone goes to that man's house to give him all their money; what was all that about? I've never seen anyone do that in Streatham.'

'I went to see that film on my first date with your mother.'

'Is that why you broke up?'

'No, it's got nothing to do with *It's A Wonderful Life*. Anyway is there anything you'll like to do today?'

'Let's go to the Streatham Common bus stop and note down all the buses that stop there, so I can record those timings.'

'Why do you want to do that?'

'The timings on the bus stops don't make any sense, so I want to double check them.'

Oh dear, I fear another car parks day coming up.

'Let's go to the cinema instead.'

'Nah, I don't like the air conditioning in the Streatham cinema. It keeps blowing into my eyes.'

'What about another cinema? Like Croydon or Brixton?'

'No way, those places turn the lights down too low when the film is on.'

I thought that was the point?

'How about I just note down the timings of the 133, 159 and 109 buses only?' Harry asks.

'OK we'll do it.'

'But you have to be fast and help me write down all the timings because if you cock it up it'll be disastrous.'

Really?

'Do you want Bernadette to come over to train you?'

'No, I'll manage.'

'After we finish at the bus stop I want to eat blueberry muffins at Neros, Costa and Pret.'

'But that's too much. What do you want to do that for?'

'I want to create a blueberry muffin spreadsheet with my markings out of ten.'

'I didn't know you liked blueberry muffins?'

'I don't.'

'So why are you going to eat so many of them?'

'I'm going to show my spreadsheet to the winner and they'll give me a lorry load of muffins free.'

As he doesn't like muffins I was going to tell him that it was a slightly pointless exercise but I thought better of it.

We arrive at the bus stop. There's half a dozen people waiting. Harry hands over a note pad to me.

'I'll let you know the bus number and the exact time it arrives at the bus stop. Just make sure that you write it down correctly.'

'I'll do my best.'

For the next couple of hours I'm frantically writing down the comings and goings of the named buses. This isn't exactly the most exciting experience that I've ever had, but I'm here with my son and that's all counts. He's loving every minute of it.

'Let me see your notes,' Harry demands.

For the next fifteen minutes he studies them intensely. I'm afraid to disturb him. He then marches over to a man holding a clipboard. He looks like some sort of bus inspector. I doubt his clipboard is as detailed as my notes.

'You lying fucking bastard,' Harry shouts at him.

'I'm sorry, can I help you?' The man replies with true British restraint, considering Harry just called him a bastard and a lying one at that.

'Let's start with the 159 bus. I've been following this bus coming into this bus stop for the last two hours and three minutes. On your bus stop it says it comes between ten and twelve minutes, well I've seen eight 159 buses come here today and the average waiting time is between thirteen and fifteen minutes. All these people waiting over there are being lied to, you scumbag.'

'OK, Harry, calm down,' I tell my son.

'The bus arrival times do sometimes vary,' the bus inspector informs Harry.

'Well you should update the bus stop timings every day if you're fucking up. The average run time on the 133 according to you is between eleven and thirteen minutes, but I worked out todays average is between fifteen and seventeen minutes. I'm going to contact the Prime Minister about this.'

'There's no need to do that,' a worried looking bus inspector replies.

'I'm sorry, my son's autistic. As you can tell he's quite passionate about this, but rest assured he won't be contacting the Prime Minister.'

The bus inspector looks relieved.

'I will. I know exactly where he lives.'

'And another thing, I noticed that three 159 buses didn't have any Metro newspapers available in them. What the hell's going on there? Do you expect the passengers to be bored out of their brains by just staring at the shitty Streatham streets? You're responsible for making the journey a fantastic experience, so make sure you fix that, OK?'

'Yes, we'll look into that.'

'And also can you employ staff to sort out the queuing system at the bus stops? Just look over there,' Harry says, pointing to the passengers waiting at the bus stop. 'The queue's a shambles. They're all over the place and that arsehole that's just arrived is waiting at the front of the queue, ahead of everyone else. He should be fined. You've got to employ staff at all the bus stops to make sure that people are queuing sequentially.'

If nothing else I'm impressed that Harry knows the meaning of the word sequentially.

'That means that the first person who arrives at the bus stop stands close to the bus stop itself. The second person to arrive at the queue has to stand behind the first person and the third person who arrives at the queue…'

'OK, Harry, I think the inspector's got the idea now.'

'I don't think so. He looks thick and is letting the queue do what the hell they like. It's chaos.'

'Well, it's good to get honest customer feedback,' the bemused bus inspector responds.

'This is my name, address and phone number. Make sure you contact me when this is all sorted,' Harry says as he hands the bus inspector a piece of paper.

Employing a member of staff to re-enforce the queuing system at every single bus stop may be a show stopper but I don't want to be a party pooper.

'Harry, I think you've made your point, let's go now.'

As Harry walks past the bus stop he gets a round of applause in appreciation of his rousing appraisal of the London Transport bus services. The only person who didn't applaud was the queue jumper.

'So what do you think of the Costa muffin?' I ask, as Harry is now writing down his muffin findings in Costa's coffee house.

'Once I have all my markings written down on the excel spreadsheet I'll think about telling you.'

I really wasn't aware that it was a matter of national security.

'Do you think that you were a bit too aggressive with that bus inspector?'

'What do you mean?'

'You did call him a lying bastard and swore at him a few times.'

'He deserved it. He's a moron and he hasn't got any hair left as well.'

Harry does seem to have a hair complex of late.

'Are you looking forward to going to Ireland?'

'Yeah, I want to swallow a few glasses of that black drink.'

'Harry, that's Guinness, and you won't like it. It's very strong.'

'But I love the black colour and it's fantastic they have the white bit at the top. That's really clever.'

Harry doesn't drink alcohol, which I'm truly grateful for. A sober Harry is enough of a challenge, can you imagine what a drunk Harry would be like?

'It's nice that your mother's coming with us isn't it?' I say.

'Does she like that leprechaun man more than you now?'

'His name's Sean and she's married to him, so yes she does love him.'

'I do remember that she got rid of us a long time ago. She was always shouting at you and sometimes at me. She hated us didn't she?'

On only a handful of occasions has Harry talked about that awful period when Laura was so ill. I cannot say how painful I feel inside that he still recalls that period. It was such a long time ago and because of his special needs I'm never sure how much he took in but it's obvious that he recollects a lot more than we thought. I've never told Laura about any such discussions with Harry. As far as she's aware it all went over his head.

'Your mum wasn't well and she definitely didn't mean all those things that she said, but she's much better now and I can tell you that she loves you more than anyone in the world.'

Harry glances up at me and then takes another bite from his blueberry muffin.

CHAPTER TWENTY-NINE: 1994

'We're keeping her in to do tests and to monitor her,' the doctor tells me.

'Did she have a breakdown?' I ask.

'Yes, she did.'

'Are you absolutely sure?'

'Yes, she has the classic symptoms – depression, acute stress disorder, extreme mood swings, unexplained outbursts, not eating properly, isolating herself, clammy hands, dizziness. I could go on.'

'I didn't mean to doubt you, I just never thought this could happen to her.'

'Given your home situation it's not all together a surprise. And it's going to be a long recovery time I'm afraid. Even when she goes home she's going to require a lot of rest and peace.'

'We're going through a difficult period right now. She wants me and my son to move out, but that's impossible right now isn't it?'

'If it's going to cause her some anxiety if you're in the house then I would suggest you do move out, but she needs someone there to keep an eye on her.'

'OK I'll arrange something. Can I see her now?'

'Yes of course, but she's heavily sedated and asleep.'

I enter her room in the hospital and am immediately taken aback at seeing my wife. She has a number of tubes attached to her, which is distressing. I sit in the chair next to the bed just staring at her, wondering how it had ever come to this?

Will I see the Laura that I loved so very much, ever again?

CHAPTER THIRTY

I've gone on a number of holidays outside the UK with Harry and his observations on other countries are interesting. Italy was 'wasting my time' as they didn't have Clover butter and France was 'pathetic' as they deliberately didn't stock Jammie Dodgers in their supermarkets. He thought that all the Irish retail people who ordered YR brown sauce couldn't spell properly and really wanted HP sauce.

'Can you believe that we're going to see the Cork carousels again?' Harry asks Bernadette as we're boarding the plane.

'No, I can't. I've waited a long time for this.'

'I wonder how many cases are going to be on those carousels? Shall we make notes and create a spreadsheet?'

'Nah, we're on holiday.'

Thanks, Bernadette. I'm so pleased that we'll soon be entering a spreadsheet free zone.

'Can you remember the last time we holidayed in Ireland?' I ask Laura.

'Oh yes. Harry was just three and we had a lovely trip. I remember saying to you at Cork airport that we've got to come back the following year. Of course we never did.'

'But we're going back now and that's all that matters.'

'It's a crazy reason why we're making this trip but I'm just so pleased that we are. It'll give us some quality time with Harry and Bernadette before the madness of next weekend. I'll be interested to hear what you have to say about the Limerick house. I value your opinion,' Laura says.

'I can't wait to see it.'

'And how are things between you and Kerry now? She left quite abruptly at our get together. Is everything OK?'

'No, far from it. She wants a divorce and has already contacted a lawyer.'

'Really? What happened?'

'I took last Wednesday off and went down to Brighton to surprise her, but she had a much bigger surprise in store for me. She told me that we've drifted apart and doesn't love me anymore. Although we've had our problems for a while now it was such a shock, and still is.'

'Wow that's unbelievable. I can't take it in. Why didn't you tell me?'

'I just couldn't bear to explain all the distressing details. You're the first person I've told.'

'And a week before the wedding?'

'Tell me about it.'

'When do you plan to tell Harry?'

'Not until we come back from honeymoon. To be honest I don't think he'll be that bothered. He was always asking her when she's going to leave anyway.'

Harry and Bernadette are sitting in the seats in front of us. Harry turns around and for a split second I thought he overheard our conversation, but no.

'I've decided I want to be a pilot. Can you buy a book on Amazon about how to get a pilot job?'

'Harry, it's not as simple as that. You have to train for years to become a pilot.'

'But if you get a good book I can skip all that crap. Wouldn't it be great when you wake up in the morning and just decide to go to Los Angeles or San Francesco? But I'm not taking these idiots with me, it'll just be me and Bernadette.' Harry says, pointing to the other passengers.

I was going to point out to my son that he had an opportunity to go to Los Angeles or San Francesco for his honeymoon but chose Halifax instead, but I don't bother.

'It's a nice idea, Harry, but it's out of the question.'

'I should ask the pilot for some training today so you won't have to spend nine pounds ninety-nine on a book. And if I get the training British Airways will probably let me fly this plane back to London on the return flight.'

'The security won't let you in to see the pilot. Now just relax and enjoy the flight.'

'Oh OK, but don't forget to buy that book. I'll read it and then become a pilot after we come back from Halifax.'

The pilot dialogue was a welcome relief from talking about the split with Kerry. I feel that Laura wants to talk more about it but she can tell from my facial expression that I don't want to. That closeness between us is still there.

'And what is the purpose of your visit?' The customs officer asks Harry.

'To video the suitcase carousels of course.'

'I'm sorry, I didn't quite catch that.'

'We came to Cork to see the suitcase carousels,' Harry re-iterates, a little louder.

The custom officer looks totally baffled, which I suppose is a normal reaction after a conversation with Harry.

'I'm sorry, my son's autistic. He's got a thing about baggage carousels,' I say.

'Hurry up and let us through, otherwise all the suitcases will be gone,' Bernadette shouts at the customs officer.

'She's autistic as well.'

A bemused custom officer waves us through.

I do remember Harry mentioning the baggage carousels when we were last here, but in the last few weeks he's talked about little else. I don't begin to understand the fascination but each to their own.

It's a short walk through customs and into the baggage reclaim area. Harry and Bernadette run ahead of us, almost knocking a couple of people over to reach their sacred destination.

'It's even better than I remembered,' a joyous Harry shouts.

A number of confused passengers stare at my son.

'There's black cases, blue cases, red cases and even a couple of pink cases; just incredible,' Bernadette adds.

Harry gets out his iPhone and starts videoing.

'Because there's only two carousels there's no cases lying all over the place with no owners. We can walk around here without tripping over all the spare cases.'

A security guard is walking nearby.

'Excuse me, sir, can I just say that your suitcase carousels are the best in the world,' Harry tells him.

'Are you taking the piss?' He replies.

'We've waited five and a half minutes so far. Do you think our cases arrive before the record of thirteen minutes and eighteen seconds from the last time we were here?'

'My son's autistic,' I tell the security guard.

'Yes, I'm sure they will,' the guard replies with a smile.

'Fucking hell, we've beaten the record. Seven minutes and twenty-six seconds. Fantastic,' Harry says as he picks up his case.

'OK let's go. I've got to pick up a car,' I say.

'No, we're going back to Streatham. My holiday's finished now.'

'Harry, we're going to our cottage in Dunmanway and spending three days there, OK?'

'Really? I thought we were coming just to see the Irish suitcases?'

'No, we're have a relaxing little break before your big day.'

'Your dad's a bit of a spoilsport, isn't he?' Bernadette tells Harry.

'Tell me about it. I didn't record the *Tom and Jerry* episode tonight cos I thought we were coming straight back. Maybe we'll be able to see it here?'

'But we won't be able to understand a fucking word they're talking about with those strange voices that they use in this country,' Bernadette proclaims. 'Anyway I better text mum to let her know that I'm not coming home today.'

'You actually told Alice that you were just coming over here to look at the suitcases?' I ask.

'Yes, of course.'

'And what did she say?'

'She just laughed. She can be a bit weird.'

It takes us an hour or so before we reach Dunmanway. This town is very special to me. My father lived here throughout his time in Ireland. My mother lived in Bandon, which is only a few miles away.

Every summer we came to this cottage for our summer holidays with my parents and my sister Fiona. All those summer memories come flooding back to me in a flash. Such happy times. Laura senses my emotions and strokes my back.

'Shall we go in?' She asks.

The familiar cottage smell engulfs me as we enter the living-room. I hope in the next couple of days that staying here will give me some much needed peace and comfort. I can almost feel my parent's presence.

'This is a bit of a shithole,' Harry proclaims.

'Harry, this was my grandparent's home, so please be more respectful.'

To some extent he has a point. It's badly in need of a lick of paint and new wallpaper in all of the rooms but I don't care one bit as it's exactly the way I remember it as a child and that in itself gives me solace.

My parents are both deceased. I was particularly close to my father. He was a kind and gentle man. Even though he passed away twenty-two years ago I often think about him. My mother was a harder person to get close to but towards the end of her life she softened and we had some special times together. However, despite their different personalities they had a very happy marriage.

'What the hell's this?' Harry says.

'What's the problem?' I ask.

'There's only a few channels and they all have this RTE sign. This bloke's talking a load of old gobbledygook,' Harry replies pointing at a TV newscaster.

'RTE is the main Irish TV channel,' I explain.

'Where's cartoon network disappeared to?'

'There's no cable TV installed. It's not worth it as hardly anybody stays here.'

'Fuck that. Let's go back to Streatham *now*.'

'Harry, we're not leaving Ireland. Just because you can't watch cartoon network. Take your case to your room and we'll decide where we'll go this afternoon.'

'Have cartoons been invented yet in Ireland?'

'Yes, Harry, they have.'

By the time we unpack our cases it's too late to venture out too far so we decide to drive into town for a meal but the first port of call is a visit to my parent's graves.

'Why did they both die? Where they fed up living with you?' Harry asks as we're standing by their graves.

'What sort of a question is that? They both had serious illnesses caused by smoking, so whatever you do don't smoke, OK?'

'That's a load of old bollocks. Clint Eastwood smoked cigars in loads of his films and he's ninety years old.'

'They're probably not real cigars.'

'Of course they are. Clint wouldn't smoke fake ones. The problem Clint had with cigars is that they made him kill a lot of people.'

'Anyway can we forget about Clint Eastwood for now? Let's just say a prayer for my parents.'

'Please God don't make my dad so grumpy,' Harry says.

Laura and I can't help but smile at each other.

Harry stays quiet for the next few minutes, which gives me the time to say some prayers. This alone was worth the trip over.

Rather than go to a restaurant we visit one of the local pubs which we've been told serves good food. There's a couple of guys with guitars playing and singing traditional Irish songs. These guys don't look like paid performers, just customers. There is also a piano in the corner of the pub and as soon as Harry notices it he takes his piano book out of his infamous backpack. His backpack is like an Aladdin's Cave. He usually has numerous DVDs, a portable DVD player, a telephone directory, which he loves reading and a few books, including his piano one. The two guys take a break, so Harry seizes his opportunity and immediately dashes across the pub to sit down at the piano.

'Hello pub. My name's Harry and I'm now going to play some proper music. I'm singing in English and if you can't understand it just ask my dad. He's the cranky man over there with no hair,' Harry says pointing at me. Now everyone in the pub is staring at me. A few of them raise their glasses to which I reciprocate.

'Looks like you're now famous in your father's town,' Laura tells me.

'Bernadette, can you come up and sit next to me?' Harry asks.

A delighted Bernadette rushes over to Harry and gets a small ripple of applause for doing so.

'Bernadette doesn't like Batman but we're still getting married in eight days' time even though the church looks like a pile of shit.'

The whole pub are now clapping and cheering Harry and Bernadette. Let's hope that the music lives up to Harry's dialogue.

'And your baggage reclaim area in Cork airport is just the best in the world.'

This also gets a warm round of applause although a few customers understandably look perplexed.

'I like Elton John cos he's got lovely hair and although it's a Friday I'm still going to play our wedding song, *Saturday Nights Alright For Fighting.*'

The customers all laugh thinking that it's a joke, but I know Harry is serious.

'We've got to get him to change his mind over that choice of song,' a worried Laura tells me.

'Yeah I'll try, but once he's made his mind up over something...'

Harry bursts enthusiastically into *Saturday Night's Alright For Fighting* with Bernadette encouraging the crowd to sing along. They're quite a double act. Harry stands up during the chorus to also urge everyone to sing *Saturday, Saturday, Saturday's Night's Alright.* After he finishes, the whole pub stands up to cheer them both. I can tell they've picked up that Harry and Bernadette are special needs, but special needs or not they deserve that standing ovation.

Harry and Bernadette stand in front of the piano and bow in unison. It's almost as if they've rehearsed it.

I wave him over and reluctantly they both come back. Quit while you're ahead.

Several people come over to us to tell us how much they enjoyed their performance. I wish Alice was here but I did video it so I'll text it across to her.

'Well that was a special moment,' a clearly emotional Laura says.

'Yes, and I'm glad we shared it together.'

She holds my hand, 'I just can't believe our son's getting married. I just never thought that would happen.'

'Nor me.'

'I can't tell you how pleased something positive is happening in his life. I've no idea how I'm going to get through the day.'

'You and me both. But it's going to be the best day yet.'

'I know I've asked you this before but please tell me the truth, does he ever talk about me not being there for him when I had the ...'

'No, he's never mentioned it. He was too young to remember it,' I lie.

'I'll never forgive myself for abandoning my son.'

CHAPTER THIRTY-ONE: 1994

'Is mummy dead?' Harry asks me.

'No, she's just resting in hospital for a while.'

It's been nearly two weeks since her hospital admission and this is our first night in our rented Streatham flat. It's already furnished but we've spent most of today travelling back and forth between the two houses carrying clothes, utensils etc. Luckily it's only a five minute drive.

In all our hospital visits Laura repeatedly told me that she wanted both Harry and me to move out of the house. I tried to reason with her but she was adamant; so here we are.

Laura's sister, Amanda, who lives in Sheffield, has arranged a leave of absence from work to look after Laura. I'm extremely grateful to her.

In recent weeks it was me who took full responsibility for Harry. It looks like this will continue for the foreseeable future or at least until Laura regains full health, which Please God she will. I've already arranged for my work hours to be reduced as I have to drop Harry at his nursery school and pick him up in the afternoon. Luckily I work locally and have been working through my lunch hours.

I worry about how this change will affect Harry. He's been even more aggressive recently. I'm getting much more kicks, punches and pinches than usual.

Another fear I have is my own health. How much longer can I continue like this? In my darkest moments I wonder if I could also be heading towards a breakdown.

And where would that leave Harry?

CHAPTER THIRTY-TWO

'So what do you like about Ireland, apart from the baggage carousels?' I ask Harry, as we're having our breakfast.

'The clouds.'

'Well there's plenty of them, but what's so special about the Irish clouds?'

'They're fluffier than the Streatham ones and they move faster.'

'OK fair enough. What else do you like about being here?'

'The rain. It's heavier than the English rain and it tickles me.'

'And the grass is darker and it's everywhere. I can't walk anywhere without seeing it. Ireland must've been the first country to have grass,' Bernadette adds.

'Did you enjoy playing the piano yesterday?' I ask my son.

'It was great, although the people were clapping too loudly.'

'Yeah that hurt my ears. They should've been more careful with their clapping,' Bernadette remarks.

I must admit I've never heard of a performer making such a compliant.

'Another thing, all those pub people seem too happy. They're all smiling and laughing. They never do that in Streatham,' Harry says.

That's probably just the Guinness effect.

'So are either of you nervous about the wedding?'

'It depends. How many people are coming to it?' Harry asks.

'At the last count it was fifty-eight, including some of your Irish relatives.'

'OK, if they all give us presents then I'm not going to get nervous.'

Most couples who are about to get married know exactly who is attending their big day, but Harry and Bernadette simply don't give a toss.

'So what are the plans for today?' Laura asks me.

'I'm hoping we'll meet up with Dermot and Liam later for a drink, but the day's free.'

'Why don't we go to Limerick today instead of tomorrow?'

'Sounds good to me. Harry, we're driving to Limerick this morning to see a house, OK?'

'I've never heard of that place, is it shit?'

'No it isn't, it's a city about ninety minutes' drive from here. Your mother wants to look at a house there.'

'But there's plenty of houses in this town, so why are we driving all the way to that strange place?'

'Harry, Sean and me are thinking of buying a house in Limerick and I want you all to have a look at it,' Laura nervously remarks.

'So you'll have two houses! That's not fair as dad only has one.'

'I might sell the Streatham house and live in Ireland with Sean.'

'Oh good, I won't have to listen to that leprechaun's voice ever again. It hurts my teeth when he talks.'

'I don't think you understand. I'll be living with Sean in Ireland.'

'Oh no, does that mean that you still have to listen to that man forever?'

Laura looks on the verge of crying so I put my arm around her.

'He clearly doesn't get it, but I'd leave it for now if I were you. Don't get too upset,' I tell her.

Laura leaves the kitchen. I don't know what she thought Harry's reaction would be but the fact that he didn't seemed concerned about her leaving the country was heart-breaking for her. Harry's acceptance of the house move will be crucial in her final decision whether to buy the property or not.

'Mister McCarthy, houses are shitty so why don't we go to the beach instead? I want to see the green sand,' Bernadette tells me.

'Yeah, houses bore the arse off me. Going to the beach is a great idea. I want to see the Irish seaweed,' Harry adds.

'OK, let me speak to your mother first, but if we go to the beach today we'll definitely be going to see the Limerick house tomorrow.'

However Harry and Bernadette walk out of the kitchen before I can finish off my speech. I end up speaking to myself, not for the first time.

Fortunately Dunmanway is only about a thirty minute drive to the seaside town of Clonakilty. Laura is quiet throughout the journey.

'Don't read too much into what Harry said earlier. I really don't think he fully grasped the situation,' I tell Laura.

'I couldn't have made it any clearer.'

'But you know how he misunderstands even the most simplest things. He's probably still thinking about the loud clapping from last night,' I say, trying to make light of it, but her worried expression hasn't shifted.

I genuinely believe that Harry doesn't realise the real possibility that Laura's moving houses and countries. Maybe once he sees the house tomorrow it'll sink in?

Although it's mid-August it's still extremely cold in this neck of the woods. Near gale force winds greet us as we head towards the beach.

Because of the inclement weather there isn't too many people on the beach, but Harry approaches a middle-aged man who's wearing speedos. Not a good look on him. He's sunbathing although I've yet to see the sun since our arrival yesterday.

'Excuse me, but what do you think of the wind?' Harry asks the man, pointing to the sky.

'I'm sorry, I don't understand?'

'Do you like the Irish wind?' He asks again, a little more aggressively.

'I've never really thought about it.'

'I saw some people over there holding onto their hats. I thought that was spectacular.'

'And I'm disappointed that the sand isn't green,' Bernadette proclaims.

'What's on the other side of the sea?' Harry inquires.

'America I suppose,' the man replies.

'Fantastic. I want to meet Tom Hanks. Let's go, Bernadette.'

With that they throw off their clothes and as they already had their swimming gear underneath they both rush towards the sea.

'Harry, don't swim too far out, it's dangerous,' I shout at my son.

'But I want to meet Tom Hanks.'

'Get back *now*,' I yell even louder.

They reluctantly return to the beach.

'You dad's a fucking spoilsport. We had a chance to meet Tom Hanks and he fucked it up for us,' Bernadette proclaims.

'I think he's just jealous that Hanks has more hair than him.'

The sunbathing speedo man probably thinks that all of this is some sort of a prank TV show, but this is reality; it's my life.

'I'm sorry about that, they're both autistic,' I say to the bemused sunbather. I'm not quite sure how much of a tan this chap will get with the sun nowhere to be seen and maybe he just enjoys hanging out in the freezing cold, accompanied by the fierce winds? Irish people are extremely robust.

Harry and Bernadette don't seem to mind. They're swimming happily and enjoying splashing each other.

'Isn't that lovely to see,' I say to Laura and for the first time since the house discussion she breaks into a smile.

'Yes it really is.'

'Are you nervous about going to the house tomorrow?' I ask.

'Yes, even more so now.'

'Has Sean been in touch?'

'Yes, I told him that we were going to see it today, so he's been texting me this afternoon.'

'Did you tell him about Harry's reaction?'

'No, I'll hold off until after we've seen the house.'

'Are you looking forward to seeing Dermot and Liam tonight?'

'David, do you mind if I give it a miss? I fancy an early night. We'll be seeing them next week.'

'You know what? I feel exactly the same. We'll go for a bite to eat around here and head home afterwards.'

'Thanks, David.'

'It's been just lovely spending some time with you. We've got on so much better in recent years, don't you think?' I say.

'Yes I do. It was all so bitter with the separation and then the divorce. I must admit I resented your close relationship with Harry and took my hostility out on you when you really didn't deserve any of it.'

'Laura, there's no need to discuss this right now.'

'Yes there is. I've got things to say that I should've said a long time ago. Not only have I been riddled with guilt at the way I let my son down I've also never got over the way I treated you all those years ago. I was the reason why we split up. I couldn't handle Harry and because of that I lost the two people I loved the most in the world. Whatever issues I was experiencing at the time you were going through the same but you held it together. Who knows what would have happened to Harry if we were both out of commission? I'm eternally grateful to you for bringing up Harry on your own. You're an amazing father and were a wonderful husband to me.'

'Laura, thanks for saying that, but there's no need. I just did what any father would've done in my position.'

For years after our separation and later divorce Laura and I had a stressful relationship. We disagreed on many issues concerning Harry. Over the years she has repeatedly expressed her guilt about Harry, but at the same time she's never really acknowledged my efforts in holding it all together during that depressing period in my life. That has always been a bone of contention with me. If anything she seemed to resent my part in Harry's upbringing and for the life of me I couldn't see why. So there was anger on both sides. My belief is that her illness had a long term impact on her mental health and it was only after she met Sean that she began to mellow. He's had such a positive effect on her.

I'm surprised but also pleased to hear her apology.

'But even when I got better Harry never wanted to stay overnight at my flat. He just wanted you.'

'That's all to do with routine. He wanted to sleep in his own bed the whole time. You know what this lot are like.'

'I know but it still hurts. It's obvious to me, and probably everyone else, that he's closer to you than me. You can't deny that.'

'Maybe he is but it's been just me and Harry under the same roof since he was four so it's understandable.'

'And will we drift further apart if I move over here?'

'No, I'll make sure that we visit regularly, I promise you that.'

'Thanks, David, that means everything to me.'

Harry and Bernadette rush over to us.

'We were just speaking to a fat man who has hair all down his back and he told us that there's a model railway village a few minutes up the road. We have to go.'

The next three hours were spent at this model railway village and I have to say it was very impressive. In addition to all the trains on display the level of detail in all the model villages was just superb.

I surprised myself at how much I enjoyed looking at trains this afternoon. Harry has loved *Thomas The Tank Engine* since he was a baby. On a daily basis I have been watching or listening to those Thomas videos and DVDs for nearly thirty years. I used to read him the Thomas books every night. All of Harry's autistic friends are also obsessed with this fictional train character. In fact at one point his school teacher asked us to wean him off Thomas as he couldn't concentrate on anything else. Yeah right, as if that was going to happen. It was during this time that one of the cartoon channels were showing back to back episodes of Thomas throughout the weekend so I rang up the cable company to ask them to block the cartoon channel for the weekend. 'But it's not showing any adult programmes' the cable guy stated. 'But they're fucking showing *Thomas The Tank Engine* episodes all weekend' was my reply.

However, Harry's reading skills picked up dramatically after he purchased virtually every Thomas book on the market, so I really should be grateful.

'Did you enjoy your day?' I ask Harry as he's getting ready for bed.

'It's in my top seven best days ever. The sea annoyed me a bit as it was too noisy but the angry wind was fantastic. It was really pissed off.'

'And what about the model railway?'

'It was the dog's bollocks. I want to get one the same size.'

'I'll see if I can get a model railway set but it'll be smaller,' I reply, knowing that we'll need a couple of acres to replicate it.

'You're being a spoilsport again. Just like when you stopped us meeting Tom Hanks.'

'OK, I'm glad that you had a good day, now give me a kiss and go to bed.'

Harry never instigates a kiss but it doesn't stop me trying. Instead he stands in front of me with our noses practically touching, just waiting for me to kiss him.

'I want a hug.'

Again he doesn't make any movement so I pull his arms around me and then kiss his forehead.

He dashes upstairs to his bedroom, no doubt to play his Thomas DVDs. Bernadette's already asleep in another bedroom.

There is one extra bedroom and that's where Laura and I will sleep, in separate beds.

'Fancy some wine?'

'I thought you'd never ask,' Laura replies.

'Have you heard from Kerry?'

'Nope.'

'Do you think she'll try to contact you before the wedding?'

'I've no idea what's going through her mind right now. I was granted a five minute audience with her when she told me our marriage was finished and she clearly didn't want to discuss it any further. As you know she texted me that evening but I haven't heard from her since. I hope that she's clever enough not to come along on Saturday, but I'll pre-empt the situation and text her this week telling her not to show up. Nothing is going to spoil Harry's big day.'

'It seems like a pretty cruel way to end a twelve year marriage. You don't think she'll agree to see a marriage counsellor?'

'No chance. To be truthful I was the one who left the coffee house first but it was obvious she had made her decision and it wasn't up for discussion. I've thought about contacting her but it's too raw right now. I also think that there's zero chance of getting back together. I've just got to try and get my head around it all.'

'And how are you dealing with it?'

'You tell me.'

'You seem angry and bitter every time I bring up her name.'

'Can you blame me?'

'Of course not, but you never know, there still might be a chance you'll get back together.'

'Thanks for being positive but it's misplaced. Anyway can we change the subject?'

'OK, when was the last time the two of us sat down together and drank wine?'

'Let me think, probably around early 1994.'

'Wow, a lot's happened since then.'

'Yeah, we've both remarried for starters. I was just so pleased when your relationship with Sean took off. He's a good guy and has always been brilliant with Harry despite the fact he calls Sean a leprechaun every time they meet up.'

'I've been so lucky.'

She looks at me as I take a gulp of my wine. 'I'm sorry, I didn't mean to sound smug…'

'I didn't think that for a minute, but do you know what I *was* thinking about recently? The day we first met.'

'Wow, what prompted that?'

'I really don't know. How much of that day do you remember?'

'About three weeks before that I split up with that arsehole, Mark, when I found out that he was cheating on me, so it was the first time I had gone out socially since then. As it was Christmas Eve I already had a few drinks before you arrived at the pub.'

'So you're saying that the only reason you agreed to go out with me was because you were pissed and on the rebound?'

'No of course not but a new relationship was the last thing I wanted at that point. I thought that you were sweet and shy, so much so that you got Alan to come over to say that you fancied me.'

'I didn't ask him to do that. I was just admiring you from a distance and he took it upon himself to approach you.'

'Well I'm glad he did. And what where your impressions of me?'

'You laughed a lot.'

'That was probably the drink.'

'I don't remember us arguing a lot before Harry was born and that sounds awful.'

'It's true. Our relationship changed. I know that we were having loads of problems with Harry even by early 1994, but it got much worse didn't it?' Laura says.

'Yes, you could say that.'

CHAPTER THIRTY-THREE: 1994

'How's she doing?' I ask Amanda.

'Not great, if I'm honest. She barely leaves her bedroom from one day to the next. I want to take her out for a walk or go shopping but she only gets out of bed for her dinner and as soon as she's finished she slopes back to her bedroom.'

'Does she eat her dinner?'

'Very little. She's skin and bones right now.'

'Has anyone from the hospital come to see her?'

'Yeah, a doctor came yesterday. He said that her lethargy is normal at this stage of her recovery. I tried to pin him down on how long the recovery period will be but he couldn't say. He said it differs too much, depending on the person.'

'Is she talking to you?'

'Just little snippets of conversation, most of which doesn't make any sense. It's been nearly two weeks since she's been home and I haven't seen any improvement. If anything I think she's retreated even more into herself these past few days. I'm worried for her.'

'Has she mentioned me or Harry at all?'

'No, not a word.'

'Amanda, I'm so grateful to you for doing this. How long have you got before you've got to go back to work?'

'I really don't know, I'll have to speak to my boss.'

'If there's any change in her can you let me know straight away, good or bad?'

'Of course I will.'

Where would I be without Amanda? She managed to get compassionate leave from her work to look after her sister, but what will happen when she has to go back to Sheffield?

I look over at Harry, who is watching a Disney video. He hasn't mentioned his mother since we've moved here, but there's no doubt it's affected him.

Normally I have to lay down next to Harry in order to get him to sleep. This is hardly ideal but needs must. As I'm usually shattered by the time my head touches that pillow I nearly always fall asleep in his bed, but yesterday he fell to sleep before me so I went into my own bed. At around three o'clock in the morning I was awoken rather abruptly when he poured a kettle full of water over my face. Luckily he didn't boil the kettle beforehand.

His pinching, punching and kicking has also increased recently, both at home and at the nursery school, so although he hasn't talked about his mother as such, his behaviour is a clear indicator that either her illness or his new living circumstances has disturbed him.

I have a long awaited psychiatrist appointment tomorrow. It can't come quickly enough.

CHAPTER THIRTY-FOUR

'Ireland has more grass than concrete,' Bernadette proclaims as we're driving to Limerick.

'I'm not sure about that,' I reply.

'I'm going to google it when we get wi-fi.'

'What time do the Irish milkmen come to all the houses?' Harry asks.

'I dunno, probably the same time they do at home.'

'Is the milk still white here?'

'Yes, it's white everywhere.'

Although Harry doesn't drink milk at all he's still obsessed about it. He's created a spreadsheet on the arrival times of the milkman every morning. He's been doing this for nearly two years and even when we went to Italy last year he got our neighbour Matthew to document these times in Harry's absence. Luckily Matthew is an early riser. The times don't vary that much, maybe a fifteen minute difference at best. After every six months he prints out a couple of copies and hands one of them to the milkman and he posts the other one to the head office. He always gets a nice thank you letter back from them which he keeps in his everything you wanted to know about milk but were afraid to ask scrapbook (as you do). The milkman, who as far as I know is not aware of Harry's autism, is more sceptical of this data, probably thinking that Harry's trying to catch him out.

'Last week I asked our milkman why he keeps giving us leaflets for eggs, bread and other drinks. He told me that's his job but I put him straight and told him you're a milkman so you should be only thinking about milk and nothing else. You're not an egg man.'

'And what did he say?'

'He just looked at me and shook his head. I know he's thick so I'll have to explain it to him again next week.'

'My milkman's always whistling when he delivers the milk, so I always tell him to shut the fuck up as I can't sleep with all that whistling racket,' Bernadette adds.

I wonder if those two milkman ever get together, over a pint of milk, to discuss their early morning encounters with their customers? If so, I'm sure Harry and Bernadette feature highly in their discussion.

'Are we nearly there yet? We've past so many houses so far. You must be so fussy about houses to skip all the others,' Harry says.

'We'll be there very soon,' I reply.

Ten minutes later we arrive at the house. An estate agent is waiting for us. His name is Timothy. He lets us in and gives us a bit of background to the area. Sean was right, it is a stunning house, three bedrooms, two bathrooms and a huge dining area. It has beautiful countryside views and just so peaceful. The only noise I can hear is the constant rain hitting the windows.

'So what do you think?' Laura nervously asks me after the guided tour.

'It's perfect. I'm sure you and Sean will be very happy here. The house has plenty of space to accommodate visitors,' I say, looking over at Harry who's in conversation with Timothy.

'Look, I love the Irish rain because it's heavier than the Streatham rain but I don't like the noise it's making on the windows. It's making my ears hurt.'

I'm sure that Timothy has heard plenty of house observations, good or bad, but I'm pretty certain that complaining about ear ache from the rain must be a first.

'I didn't see any ants in the garden, are they visiting another house?' Harrys asks Timothy.

'I'm sorry, my son's autistic,' I say.

'No problem, I'll wait outside to give you some privacy,' he replies, obviously willing to get soaked rather than listen to Harry talking about rain ear ache and the activities of the Limerick ants.

'How much is this house going for, if you don't mind me asking?' I ask Laura.

'500,220.'

'And how much is Sean's place worth?'

'At least 700,000.'

'A nice profit and you still have your Streatham flat.'

'Yes, financially it all makes sense. If you were in my shoes what would you do?'

'Don't put me on the spot like that, Laura. That's impossible for me to answer.'

'Yeah I know. I'm sorry.'

'It all comes down to Harry, doesn't it?'

'Of course.'

'If you do decide to move you're obviously going to sell Sean's house but what about taking back your flat once the current rental agreement expires? It'll give you a good base and you'll be close to Harry. The best of both worlds?'

'Yes, I thought about that but do I want to spend all my time going back and forth? I'm sure that Sean doesn't want to do that all the time in his retirement and I don't want to spend too much time away from him. I know it's completely different circumstances but I've seen what happened to you and Kerry.'

'Yeah I understand that.'

'Let me ask Harry again,' Laura nervously says.

'Harry, do you like this house?' She asks.

'I don't like the noise the rain makes on the windows, but I do like the rain.'

'OK, apart from the rain do you think that the house is nice?'

'Because it's a big house I haven't been bumping into people, cos that hurts my shoulder. But the ceilings are too high and I don't like the pink soap in the bathroom.'

'So it's good that your shoulders will be OK here, but is there anything else you like?'

'I had a crap in the upstairs toilet and it flushed my shit away really quickly.'

'Sean and me might move here permanently. That means we'll sell Sean's Streatham house and live all the time in Ireland. Do you understand?'

'Is it because of the brown carpet stairs in his house?'

'No, we just want to live here. You and Bernadette can come anytime you want and I'll still travel to Streatham a lot. Does that sound OK?'

'Will you have the Disney channel in this joint?'

'Yes.'

'Can I bring my Thomas DVDs with me?'

'Absolutely. In fact I'll buy you loads of them over here so you won't have to keep on bringing them over with you.'

'Nah, don't bother. I won't be able to understand a fucking word Thomas is saying with that strange accent.'

'Alright then, I'll buy some in Streatham and keep them in here.'

'That'll be great and then you can watch them when that leprechaun man's voice drives you bonkers.'

'Hold on, can you get UK Gold here because I have to see Ted Rodgers in 321?' Bernadette asks.

'Yes, we've got UK Gold.'

'OK, you can buy this house now,' Bernadette announces, with Harry nodding in agreement.

The look of delight on Laura's face is priceless.

'So has that made your mind up?' I ask.

'It's certainly a big obstacle out of the way. I was too caught up with Harry's reaction to think that it could become a reality, but now he's given me the green light I have to make a decision sooner rather than later.'

Throughout the journey back Laura was quiet. I didn't want to discuss it any further. It's up to her now.

The next morning we're on the London-bound plane.

'Did you enjoy your time in Ireland?' I ask Harry.

'Yeah, I love it when it pisses down with rain. The Streatham weather is going to be sunny today with no clouds, so that's really fucked me off big time.'

'Plus it's going to take me about eight days to get over that Irish jet lag illness,' Bernadette adds.

'Did you enjoy the break?' I ask Laura.

'It was wonderful, just like old times.'

'Yes it was and you know what I'm going to contact Kerry to see if she'll meet up. I know that it's extremely doubtful that anything will come of it but what have I got to lose?'

'Good to see that Ireland's had a positive effect on you.'

'And only five days to go before the big day. Don't forget the rehearsal on Thursday.'

'As if. I'm so looking forward to everything, but I still feel nervous at the same time.'

'Yeah, me too. But we'll draw strength from each other and just for a day or two we'll be a family again.'

CHAPTER THIRTY-FIVE: 1994

'I'm really sorry to hear about Laura. What's the latest on her?' Carol asks.

'She's home with her sister, Amanda. I'm in touch with Amanda every day. It looks like it's going to be a long, slow recovery.'

'And how are you coping with it?'

'I'm really struggling if I'm totally honest. I can't believe what's happening to Laura. She went downhill fast.'

'I think it's been building up for some time and has just hit her all at once.'

'A couple of days before she went into hospital she got really angry about something or other, I'm not even sure what. She started shouting about Harry being totally responsible for her ill health and Harry was in the room listening to her. It was just awful.'

'Did Harry react?'

'No, not at all. He just stared at her. I've no idea how much of it he took in. Do you think he would've understood any of it?' I ask Carol.

'I don't really know. Obviously he picked up on her anger but how much he comprehended is questionable. It can't have been nice for you and Harry to hear that but please don't take it too much to heart as she's sick and not fully accountable for her actions. You just said that you're struggling, can you give me an example?'

'I just feel tense and depressed the whole time. I'm so worried about Laura and I'm also trying to look after Harry on my own. I'm also concerned that I may be heading down the same path as Laura. I just feel like I can't cope but I have to, it's as simple as that. What choice have I got?'

'Have you talked to your doctor about taking medicine to calm your nerves?'

'That's going to be a last resort. I saw how depleted Laura became after taking the medicine for a couple of weeks. She was just so lethargic and seemed to lose interest in everything, including her own family.'

'Do you get any respite?'

'You're kidding. We've never had any respite since Harry was born. Because of Harry's issues we couldn't just ask your average teenager to baby sit. It's always been just Laura and me and now just me.'

'Before we talk about Harry I just want to ask you more about Laura. You're understandably concerned for her but if you don't mind asking, what sort of a future do you now envisage with Laura?'

'These sessions are all about Harry, so why is that relevant?'

'I'm sorry if it may sound too personal but your answer will give me a good insight into your current mental health and of course that will have an impact on Harry.'

'I do have serious doubts about whether we'll ever get back together. Before Harry was born we had such a special relationship. We did everything together. We loved going to the theatre, concerts, pubs, museums and holidays abroad. We had a lot of the same interests. Some of our friends told us that we were the perfect match. When Harry was born we were both so excited. I remember when he was a couple of months old we went on holiday to Ireland. My parents were Irish and most of my relatives still live over there. We received so many lovely compliments about Harry, even from strangers in the street. It was a fantastic trip. While we were over there we were talking about having another child sooner rather than later. We wanted Harry to have a brother or sister. Most new parents struggle at the beginning with the lack of sleep but from day one Harry had no interest in sleeping. As I've told you already he can get by with only a couple of hours kip. The initial sleep deprivation has continued to the present day. I've got used to the lack of sleep but it does make me edgy and as both Laura and I were in the same boat our relationship has consequently suffered, there's no question about that. Harry's issues have had a big impact on us. Sometimes we've had different views on how to deal with his behaviours. I'm more laid back than Laura and I would let Harry get away with some of his aggressive actions whereas Laura would always pull him up straight away. In retrospect, I think her approach was correct but it led to disagreements. Harry's just so different from any other child and we just didn't know what to do. I'm really sorry for rambling on but in answer to your question I do think that my marriage is on the verge of collapse, but I hope and pray that I'm wrong.'

'Thanks for being so honest. That must've been hard for you.'

'I actually feel better for getting it off my chest. I haven't told that to anyone else; in that much detail anyway.'

'And can you tell me about the impact Laura's illness and moving house has had on Harry?'

'On the day we moved house he actually asked if Laura was dead.'

'Oh wow and what did you say?'

'I tried to reassure him that she's not well right now but she'll get better.'

'Did that calm his fears?'

'I don't know. He just walked out of the room. I tried talking to him again about it but I got no response.'

'Have you noticed any difference in his behaviour recently?'

'He's become more aggressive. As you know, I have to lay down with him at night and although he doesn't usually settle he rarely hits me but in the last couple of weeks he's been pinching me when we're in bed together. It's gone up another level as you can see,' I hand over the latest physical assault stats.

'Wow, that's at least doubled. Have you tried letting him go to bed on his own?'

'Yes, loads of times but he gets really angry and literally pulls me back into his bedroom.'

'Did Laura ever lay down with him?'

'No, it's always been me, but that's nothing against Laura, it's just Harry's routine. She did try a few times but he pushed her away. He only ever wanted me.'

'So there's no escape from the physical assaults, even at night time?'

'No escape whatsoever.'

'How's he getting on at his nursery?'

'It's following the same pattern. Harry seems to be fighting the other kids almost every day. I had the parents of one child, that Harry assaulted, come around to my house yesterday to have a go at me.'

'That must've been distressing.'

'You're not kidding. I apologised to them and tried to explain Harry's issues but they weren't interested and told me that he should be chucked out of the nursery school. They've already put in a complaint against him, so it's probably only a matter of time.'

'That's the last thing you need right now.'

'Absolutely, but Harry has hit this kid before, so I suppose I can't blame them.'

'Would you've done the same in their circumstances?'

'I'd like to think I wouldn't, but who knows?'

'How did you feel after they left?'

'I cried. Despite knowing that Harry is the instigator I just felt so sorry for him. He obviously can't control it and needs help. I also felt sorry for the boy and his parents. No parent wants their kid bullied.'

'Is Harry always the instigator?'

'Yes, as far as I can tell. It's usually something stupid like he didn't like the way the other kid was dressed or playing with his toys. It doesn't make any sense to me.'

Carol continues to write everything down.

'This is turning into quite a session. Are you sure my times not up?'

'Don't worry about it, my next client is not due for another half an hour.'

'I do have a question for you. Why haven't you wanted to see Harry? Surely that will help you?'

'In cases like yours it's best to gather all the information about Harry before even considering seeing him.'

'Do you mean you're not sure if you ever want Harry to come to any future session?'

'At this point I just don't know. But rest assured it's common practice.'

'I'm surprised, I just thought that you'd definitely want to see him.'

'I've got a very good picture of Harry, thanks to you and Laura.'

'In our last session you were implying that you were close to another diagnosis for Harry. Any conclusion on that?' I ask Carol.

'No, not yet.'

'And you're not willing to say anything about it?'

'No, because I could be wrong. The majority of cases that I deal with can be diagnosed in the first session but this has not proved to be the case with Harry. I need a few more meetings with you. I'm sure you can understand that.'

'Yes, of course. I didn't want to pressurise you in any way.'

'It's been a very fruitful session. Can you book an appointment for next week?'

'No problem. Apologies if I talked more about me than Harry today.'

'It all helps.'

I make my way to Harry's nursery school. I feel in a better frame of mind after talking to Carol about my relationship with Laura in some detail, although the conclusion was hardly encouraging.

CHAPTER THIRTY-SIX

'You're really not going to have *Saturday Nights Alright For Fighting* as your wedding song?' I ask Harry as he tucks into his Frosties, without milk.

'Of course. It's a great song and everyone can sing along to it like all those smiley Guinness people did.'

'But normally the song should be a slow romantic song, just for you and Bernadette.'

'What about *Ernie (The Fastest Milkman In The West)*?'

'The Benny Hill song?'

'Yeah, he was so funny. He was born on the twenty-first of January nineteen twenty-four and snuffed it on the twentieth of April nineteen ninety-two. I loved it when he slapped that bald man on the head.'

'Harry, that song isn't appropriate.'

For both of my marriages I didn't even consider a wedding song about a milkman delivering milk very quickly and shagging women along the way. Maybe that's where it all went wrong?

'But Bernadette loves that song.'

'Have you talked to her about your choices?'

'Yeah she loves them both. Don't you like Benny Hill?'

'He was a great comedian but he wasn't the best singer,' I reply.

'It's a shame he died cos he would've made the greatest best man ever and he could've slapped you on your bald head.'

It seems that everyone, dead or alive, would have been Harry's preferred best man.

I know it's late in the day but I don't think Harry knows exactly what getting married entails. We've only briefly discussed how he feels about living full time with Bernadette. Harry, like a lot of autistic people, is extremely self-centred. He is selfish but not in a malicious way; it just comes with autism. Bernadette is the same, so as the wedding day is nearly upon them I'm thinking more and more how they'll adjust to their new circumstances.

Harry doesn't seem the least bit nervous about the wedding apart from getting to the pork pies before the guests. I'm far more anxious, especially right now with the subject matter I'm about to discuss with him.

'Harry, I know that we've talked about sex a few times before but do you know everything about it now?'

'Yeah, no problem.'

'Can you explain it to me?'

'Why? Have *you* forgotten it?'

'No, but I want you to tell me what *you* know about sex.'

'It's just like all those Carry On films when Sid James is always looking at the women's knockers.'

'Well that's part of it. But can you give me more detail?'

'I just need to get my todger out, that's all.'

'OK, and what do you do with your penis out?'

'That's a fantastic word, it makes me laugh.'

'What happens when you get your penis out?' I reiterate.

Harry starts laughing.

'This is serious, Harry. Just tell me what you know.'

'I just have to stick my todger up her leg. It'll know what to do from there.'

I've never quite heard that description before but I think he's got the gist.

'Do you and Bernadette want babies?' I ask. We talked about this before and he seemed quite negative about the baby prospect and I want to delve a bit further.

'Fuck off. They piss and shit everywhere and I'm not cleaning that up and neither is Bernadette. Plus when they get a bit older they're going to take all my Thomas DVDs.'

All good reasons.

'Have you talked to Bernadette about having babies?'

'Yeah, she thinks they're little shits and as they can't wash the dishes she's not interested.'

So for the fact that babies can't wash the dishes, in addition to constantly pissing, shitting and nicking Harry's Thomas DVDs probably means that I won't become a grandfather. Oh well…

Harry wanders off to the living-room while I'm thinking about what to do with him today. I'm not sure I can stand another car park, bus stop or blueberry muffin tasting day right now.

I decide to follow up on my promise to Laura and ring Kerry. She answers straight away.

'How are things? We haven't spoken since…'

'I'm OK.'

'Did you contact your lawyer?'

'Yes I did.'

'And?'

'I just met him a couple of days ago and told him all about us, but don't worry I won't be seeking anything from you. I want the break up to be as quick and pain free as possible.'

'Does that mean I can keep your Ed Sheeran CDs?' I ask, attempting a touch of humour into the conversation.

'David, I'm really sorry about the way I told you. I've been thinking about ending our marriage for such a long time and was going to wait a few months but the whole situation was killing me and I just blurted it out. I feel awful about it.'

'At the risk of repeating myself don't you think we should give it another go? Maybe go and see a marriage counsellor?' I ask, almost in desperation.

'I just don't love you anymore and before you ask again I'm not involved with anyone else. My total focus right now is with Niall. I shouldn't have sent you that lawyer text so soon, that was a mistake. I just want everything finalised as quickly as possible so I can get on with my life.'

'With Harry getting married and retirement not that far away don't you think we should wait and see what happens? I'll have more time on my hands.'

'That won't change a thing and I'm really sorry about the timing of this, just before the wedding. It wasn't planned that way.'

'You're not coming to the wedding, are you?'

'No, I don't want anything to distract from Harry's big day.'

A bit too late for that.

'The lawyer told me that if nothing is contested the divorce should be finalised in six months,' she adds.

Before this conversation there was a very small part of me that thought we could give our relationship another go. I now know that our marriage is dead, or will be in six months' time. I don't know what the top ten reasons for a marriage break up are but I would imagine having an affair would be up there, along with an abusive relationship, financial trouble, some form of addiction, etc, but in our case it's a question of living separate lives due to the lack of home care for special needs adults. I'm not saying that our lives were perfect before Kerry and Niall moved to Brighton, it was stressful but we learnt to cope with that, most of the time anyway. The majority of parents with two autistic sons would feel the strain, but in my mind anyway it was a never a question of splitting up. That all changed with the Brighton move.

I was pleased that we were at least civil to each other in our telephone conversation and she didn't object to me keeping her Ed Sheeran CDs.

So where do I go from here? As we've been living apart for the last eighteen months nothing feels too different right now. Kerry's already taken at least half of her belongings to Brighton, so I think it'll only take one trip to bring the rest down. I wonder if she'll do this when I'm in sunny Halifax to avoid meeting me. Who knows when I'll see her again?

'Was that the Irish chick on the phone? You know the one who never stops talking.' Harry says.

'Yes, and her name is Kerry. In fourteen years you've *never* called her by her name. Not once. Why's that?'

'Cos it's a crazy name and I'm not getting involved with it.'

That's cleared that one up.

'Does she live with that old bird?'

'That's her mother. No, she's at home with Niall.'

'She's still with him?'

'Of course, Niall's her son.'

'I thought she might have got fed up with him cos he can't be arsed to talk.'

I've had similar discussions a millions times previously so I'm not in the mood to discuss it any further. However, there is one thing I do want to tell Harry.

'I was going to wait until after the wedding but I might as well tell you now. Kerry and I are splitting up, we're getting a divorce.'

'Is it because you've got no hair left?'

'No it isn't.'

'Oh I know, she's finally found a handsome man?'

'No, we've just drifted apart. We don't love each other anymore.'

Half of that last sentence is true.

'This is the ninth happiest day of my life. I fucking hated it when she sneezed, it was too loud and hurt my ears. Can I sell her clothes on eBay? I need some dosh to buys loads of skittles.'

'No, you can't sell her clothes.'

'Oh OK,' Harry replies with a despondent expression as he walks back into the living room.

He's obviously more disappointed that he hasn't profited from the end of my marriage, rather than expressing any level of sympathy towards his father. Nevertheless, it's the reaction I expected and I'm glad that I got it out of the way.

I've no idea what to do today so against my better judgement I ask my son.

'I want to go to London,' Harry says.

'OK, that sounds good. And where do you want to go once we're there?'

'Nowhere.'

'What do you mean?'

'On the journey into London Victoria train station I want to get into the first carriage and count the number of people who get in and leave at every stop.'

'And don't tell me, you're going to put this on a spreadsheet?'

'Of course.'

'And what are you going to do with this spreadsheet?'

'Can you just wait until I tell you my plan? Once the train arrives at Victoria station we'll get straight back on another train to Streatham Common. We'll get into the first carriage again and count the people getting in and leaving. I know that you're slow as fuck old man, but you've got to be quick to get into that first carriage as it's the most popular carriage on the train and if we don't get on it my plan collapses.'

'I'll do my best.'

'I have to compare the differences between the inward and outward journeys. Once we're back at Streatham Common station we'll get on the Victoria train but this time we'll get into the second carriage. Now you can't piss around because the second carriage is the second most popular carriage, OK?'

'Don't worry, I won't let you down.'

'You better not. And once we get to Victoria we'll get on the second…'

'It's alright, I think I know where this is going.'

'I also want to chat to some of the passengers to find out their thoughts on trains and other stuff.'

I know from past experience that it's a waste of time giving Harry alternatives. At least I'll be sitting down this time.

'I'm going to send my spreadsheet to Southeastern railway and they'll probably give me a free train ticket for the rest of my life.'

I really have to manage his expectations on this one.

I can't imagine too many prospective grooms, with the wedding only a matter of days away, spending all their time counting train passengers getting in and out of specific train carriages. Let me modify that statement – I can't imagine *anybody* spending their time counting train passengers getting in and out of specific train carriages. But that's what it's like living in Harry's world.

Despite Harry's scepticism we manage to get on the first carriage at Streatham Common station. The true test will be trying to do the same at Victoria station.

I settle next to Harry in an excellent vantage point for viewing the commuters' comings and goings.

'This is going to be one of my greatest ever achievements,' an excited Harry blurts out.

'What do you mean?'

'It's twenty minutes from Streatham Common station to London Victoria. Six minutes from Streatham Common to Balham, two minutes from Balham to Wandsworth Common, four minutes from Wandsworth Common to Battersea Park and four minutes from Battersea Park to Victoria. I really have to be in the zone today.'

'I've never heard you use the *in the zone* expression before?'

'Arthur Ashe said it first about that other tennis bloke, Bjorn Borg on the twenty-second of February nineteen seventy-four.'

'Are you making this up?'

'No, those American TV commentators are always banging on about it in their football matches. I love Americans because of their shiny teeth and smiles but those commentator arseholes never stop fucking talking and it's all a load of old bullshit and it gives me a headache. But I still like being in the zone.'

I google Harry's Arthur Ashe claim and sure enough after being defeated by Borg he said about his opponent that 'he is in what we call the zone' and it's one of the first times this expression was used in this context. Harry has an almost photographic memory for things that interest him. It's usually birthdays of actors and musicians and conversations that I had several years ago. Although the zone anecdote is somewhat obscure I'm still very impressed.

'I really like Arthur Ashe. It's a shame he's dead cos I would've…'

'Yes, I know, you would've asked him to be your best man.'

'Seven people in and two people left. What's the point of getting off at Balham? It's shit,' as we stop at Balham station.

'Harry, that's great but can you just write it down rather than tell me? And if need be I'll look at it later.'

No chance of that.

'Sourpuss.'

'What do you think of trains?' Harry asks a commuter sitting opposite us.

'What do you mean?'

'Are you English?'

'Yes.'

'So what's the matter with you? Are you ill?'

'Harry, don't be so rude. I'm sorry, my son's autistic. He's doing a train survey,' I explain to the confused commuter.

'Hurray up mate, we've only got seventy-eight seconds before Wandsworth Common station.'

'Can you be a little more specific about your question?' He asks.

'Oh fuck off. You're wasting my time and destroying my day.'

Seventy-eight seconds later we arrive at Wandsworth Common station. Harry frantically writes down the latest stats. Another passenger sits opposite us.

'What do you think of trains?' Harrys asks the new victim, I mean arrival.

'I don't understand?'

'Not again. You lot are shitting clueless. You don't deserve to travel on trains. Look I've only got three minutes and thirty-two seconds before we get to Clapham Junction. I'll ask you again – do you like trains?'

'Well, I suppose so.'

'Why?'

'Because they get me to my place of work.'

'And that's all?'

'Yeah.'

'Do you like today's train driver?'

'I've never met him.'

'Fucking hell, he's taking you to work and you don't even know who he is?'

The usual perplexed expression appears from anyone talking to Harry for even a short period of time.

'When was the last time you tipped the train driver?'

'I've never tipped any train driver.'

'You bastard.'

'OK, Harry, cut out the swearing.'

'But those tossers don't give a fuck about trains.'

'All they want to do is have a bit of peace and quiet on their train journey, OK?' I tell my son.

When we arrive at London Victoria Harry pushes past a couple of people to get to the driver as he steps onto the platform.

'What a fantastic journey. I really enjoyed the way you drove that train; just amazing,' Harry tells the driver.

'Err, thanks,' came the bemused reply.

'I thought it was just so spectacular when you told everyone to look out for suspicious bags. Are you a policeman in your spare time?'

'No, just a train driver. Normally the guards make the announcements, but our guard was sick today.'

'Guards are a fucking a waste of space. I clapped when you said that. Was that an ad-lib?'

'No, it's mentioned every day.'

'And I loved it when you were told everyone that all the London Underground trains were running OK. The passengers needed to know that, but I'll be honest with you not one of those fuckers were even listening to you. If I bring down my Thomas the Tank Engine DVD covers next week can you sign them?'

'Don't worry, my son's autistic,' I say to the driver.

Harry seems to have forgotten that he'll be on his honeymoon next week.

'What a professional hey Dad?' Harry says, pointing at his hero.

'Yes he is.'

'Well, give him a tenner,' Harry demands.

'I'm not sure that's the done thing.'

'Give him a tenner or I'll drop you as best man and ask H from Steps.'

'Mate there's no need to do that, it's just my job,' the driver tells me.

'But it's the best fucking job in the world. I was originally thinking of becoming a pilot but now it's got to be a train driver. It's easier cos I won't have to wear a tie.'

I hand Harry a ten pound note. He carefully folds it up and places it behind the driver's ear. He's obviously been watching old films and noticed that's the traditional cigarette holding area.

The train driver shakes Harry's hand. He seems genuinely pleased that someone has appreciated his work. That was lovely to see.

We go through the ticket barrier and Harry notices that the next train to Streatham Common is in two minutes, so we rush back through the barrier and Harry manages to claim the last available seat, leaving me standing. But then a teenage girl offers her seat to me which I decline. I thought it was a kind gesture but it also confirmed that I'm at the stage of my life when I'm being offered seats on trains because of my age. I'm only sixty, do I look older than that?

'Do you think they should serve fry ups on the morning Southeastern trains?' Harry asks a passenger.

'That's a great idea. I'll vote for that.'

Harry writes down his response.

'But who's going to wash up the dishes?' The passenger asks.

'The ticket collector of course. His job only lasts for twenty minutes every day. All he does is ask passengers if they've got tickets, well they're always going to have tickets otherwise they won't be able to get through the Victoria station ticket barriers. So the ticket collector's got another seven hours to do the dishes.'

'You're brilliant. You've got it all sussed out,' the deluded passenger replies.

'I happen to be in the zone right now.'

I look at my son and it fills me with joy to see his happy expression. Admittedly, his happiness stems from his idea that Southeastern Railway will introduce fry up breakfasts on the commuter trains with the ticket collector doing the washing up. I know that Southeastern Railway wouldn't implement this in a million years and I'm sure that the railway trade unions might have a thing or two to say about the new ticket collector duties.

'Would you like music played on the trains in the morning?' Harry asks an elderly man.

'Oh no, I like it peaceful.'

'What about any of those dead singers that Dad likes?'

'Like who?'

'That geezer who always wore suits. Dad calls him Sinatra. Even though he's brown bread they keep on playing his music everywhere, even in Neros, but he can't claim any dosh for it. If he was alive he'd be gutted about that.'

It's that Harry logic again.

'Have you heard of that bloke?'

'Yes, I'm aware of Frank Sinatra.'

'I think you'll like him cos it looks like you'll be snuffing it soon as well. Have you got a date for your funeral?'

This remark brings a few sniggers from some of the passengers and even the elderly man smiles.

'I like Sinatra. His music is timeless, so yes, playing his songs on the train would be just fine,' the elderly man replies.

So while we're tucking into our fry ups we can now listen to Frank on our morning commute into London. Job done.

We make four trips back and forth from Streatham Common to London. Harry is delighted because he managed to note down all the passenger activities in addition to conducting quite a number of 'interviews'.

After dinner Harry retreats to his bedroom while I open a can of lager and switch on the TV. Although I'm staring at the television I've no idea what show is on. My mind drifts back to a Friday afternoon six months ago.

CHAPTER THIRTY-SEVEN: SIX MONTHS PREVIOUSLY

'How was your week?' I ask as my son gets into my car.

'On Tuesday the HP sauce bottle was nearly empty and it made the squeaking noise which makes me go mad. I asked one of those staff people if I could have a full bottle instead and they told me to finish the empty one off first. So I went into the toilet and put toilet paper in my ears so I didn't have to hear the HP racket.'

'Alright, apart from the HP sauce incident was everything else OK?'

'The rubbish men arrived thirteen minutes late yesterday, that really pissed me off, but they did collect everything.'

'Why are you interested in the timings of the rubbish collection? It doesn't matter what time they arrive.'

'It fucking does. They're supposed to come at eight-thirty and I can't take my shower until they come, so when they're late it wastes my time.'

'You didn't tell them off again?'

'I opened my bedroom window and told them if they don't arrive on time next week I'm going to contact the army and get them to do it instead.'

'And what did they say?'

'The man just waved at me and smiled.'

'Anyway, I've got your dinner in the oven. It's your favourite - burger, chips and beans.'

'How many chips did you do this time?'

'Twenty-three as usual.'

'The burger isn't a pig colour, is it?'

'No it's well done, just the way you like it.'

Thirty minutes later Harry is happily scoffing through his twenty-three chips when my phone rings. It's Alice.

'Hi ya, what's up?' I ask.

'I just can't believe it. Just amazing news.'

'What is?'

'Stop messing with me.'

'I'm sorry, you've completely lost me?'

'You don't actually know, do you?'

'Know what?'

'Harry and Bernadette are engaged.'

'Alice, have you been drinking that red wine again? I told you it's much stronger than you think it is.'

'Just ask him now.'

'Harry, are you engaged to Bernadette?'

'Yep,' he casually replies as he takes another bite from his burger.

'Alice, let me ring you back.'

'When the hell did this happen?'

'At twelve minutes past three this afternoon.'

'I picked you up at three-thirty and you didn't say anything to me about it?'

'I thought that you'd be more interested in my HP sauce problem.'

'OK, after you told me how you overcame the HP sauce crisis didn't you think of letting your father know that you got engaged?'

'No, because I kept on thinking about those rubbish blokes being late and I couldn't get it out of my brain. Anyway, Friday is the only day of the week that you drink wine and I didn't want to tell you when you're pissed cos you'll be crying and I couldn't be arsed with all that crap.'

Harry's right, it's only on Fridays that I have a couple of glasses of wine (not enough to get pissed). Is this my own OCD behaviour that Harry has also inherited?

'So how did you propose?'

'She broke off half of her Kit Kat and gave it to me so I asked her to marry me.'

'Has she ever given you her Kit Kat before?'

'Yeah, loads of time, but it's usually only one piece; this was the first time that she gave me two pieces.'

'And that was the reason you asked her to marry you?'

'She must really like me if she wants to give me fifty percent of her Kit Kat.'

'And what did she say?'

'She said 'that's fantastic' and then left to meet up with her mum.'

'And how did you feel after she was gone?'

'I felt great. The Kit Kat was really nice cos it had been in the fridge for over thirteen hours. She'd only give me a soft Kit Kat in emergencies.'

'And what do you think about the prospect of being married to Bernadette?'

'She's been my best friend for fourteen years, five months and seventeen days and just loves Thomas, so as long as she doesn't snore at night I'm happy to get married.'

CHAPTER THIRTY-EIGHT: 1994

'We've covered Harry's aggression in some detail in the last few sessions, so I want to discuss some of his other behavioural traits today,' Carol tells me.

'OK, sounds good.'

'I know that his language is limited but does he ever instigate conversations with you?'

'No not really. Sometimes he'd say I want chips but that's more of a demand. He never asks me any questions.'

'When he's playing with his toys does he ever engage with you?'

'Never.'

'Do you try to play games with him?'

'Do you mean with his toys?'

'Yes.'

'I've tried but every time I pick up one of his toys he snatches it back.'

'Does he still have difficulty making eye contact with you?'

'He hardly ever looks at me.'

'Has he got any friends?'

'No, he's very insular. Because of his aggressive behaviour at the nursery school all the kids are afraid of Harry and don't go anywhere near him, which I perfectly understand, but it pains me to see how his behaviour has alienated everyone.'

'Is Harry routine driven?'

'Oh yes.'

'Can you give me an example?'

'If I'm driving to the supermarket for instance and I take a couple of side roads to avoid the traffic he gets really annoyed and bangs me across the head with a book or video.'

'Does that happen every time you take a different route to a familiar place?'

'Yes, without fail. What does that mean?' I ask, but Carol continues to make notes. When she stops writing she puts the pen and pad on a side table and continues to stare at the writing pad.

'Is everything OK?'

'I'm going to refer him for tests to confirm that he has ODD, OCD and ADHD, but I'm now convinced that Harry is on the autistic spectrum.'

'Why do you think that?'

'No eye contact, no social interaction, very routine driven, limited speech and unwarranted aggression. For the past few weeks I'd been thinking about the autistic diagnosis constantly but I wanted to hear more from you before I truly convinced myself. I'm ninety percent sure that he has Aspergers at the very least.'

'That's at the more able end of the autism spectrum?'

'Yes it is, but the only way of finding out is getting an appointment at Guys hospital. They will conduct a series of structured tests and will able to tell you the outcome within an hour or two. The autistic consultants at Guys are amongst the best in the UK. I know that this comes as a shock to you but early intervention is a good thing. You'll be able to get him into an autistic pre-school setup which will be more suitable to his needs. However, I'm jumping the gun right now. If I put my referral through today you should get an appointment within a couple of weeks. How do you feel about this?'

'To be honest I'm stunned. I've been down to the library recently and looked at some books about behavioural management and autism was mentioned. Although some autistic behaviours were very similar to Harry's there were a lot that weren't, so for some reason I didn't think it was applicable. I was obviously wrong. I really don't know too much about autism, apart from that film with Dustin Hoffman.'

'Rain Man.'

'Yes, that's it.'

'The media tend to say that autistic people always have a special talent, like they can draw the world map just by memory or solve complex mathematical equations in seconds. From my limited experience the reality is very different, but I'm no expert on autism and that's why we need to get Harry tested as soon as possible.'

'It sounds like you've had some experience dealing with this. Does Harry fall into the same behavioural traits as your other clients?'

'As you've just said there are many differences but also a lot of similarities. When do you plan to tell Laura?'

'It's pointless, it'll just go over her head.'

My head is spinning as I leave Carol's office. My whole world has just been turned upside down.

CHAPTER THIRTY-NINE

It's four o'clock in the morning and I'm sitting in the kitchen drinking my second cup of coffee. I didn't sleep well last night mainly because I was worrying about the wedding. I'm concerned that Harry doesn't seem to be taking the occasion seriously. He seems oblivious to it. Is he aware of the responsibilities of marriage? Given his autism that's an unfair question. Ever since his engagement he really hasn't talked at all about the wedding. His casual attitude is unnerving and from my understanding Bernadette is pretty much the same.

My overnight thoughts also included Kerry. Although our last telephone conversation was civil, I'm still angry about the discussion in Brighton that ended our marriage so abruptly. Why did I not see this coming? And why couldn't she at least agree for us to see a marriage counsellor to talk about our problems? Surely a twelve-year-old marriage was worth that extra effort?

Maybe she thinks differently but my attitude towards her hasn't changed much over the years. I've always tried my best to consider her feelings and her point of view even when I was attacked on a daily basis by Niall. He was constantly punching me in the testicles which meant I had to wear a cricket box for nearly two years. That was extremely uncomfortable and gave me skin rashes in my nether regions. He also pinched my arms and ears, head-butted me regularly and often gave me a kick in the shins. Although this understandably got me down I never once retaliated, either physically or verbally. I just knew that Niall couldn't help his OCD behaviour. To be fair, Kerry always praised me for my tolerance and patience with Niall.

The thought of going through another divorce is just heart-breaking.

Even after the Halifax trip I've still got some leave to take so I'm thinking of taking a break on my own. Harry will be with Bernadette most weekends so this frees me up. A week in New York or California sounds ideal. I've never gone on a holiday on my own. When I was growing up holidays were always with my parents and my sister Fiona, then Harry and Laura and lastly Harry, Kerry and Niall. The more I think about it the more I'm coming around to the idea. It'll probably feel quite strange not travelling with Harry but it might be liberating. It's exactly what I need right now.

The rehearsal is at six o'clock tonight but what will the rest of the day consist of? In the past couple of weeks we've travelled into London to see Lee Mack only to promptly return home because of Lee's beard. We've spent an afternoon in various car parks in South London noting down how much petrol the drivers still had left in their car etc. We've visited a Streatham bus stop to check the timings of the buses and to point out to an inspector that he should have a staff member at every stop to monitor the bus queue. And lastly we travelled back and forth from Streatham Common to Victoria checking the number of passengers coming out of all stations on this route. Harry is also going to suggest to Southeastern Railways that they should have fry ups on the morning commutes with the ticket collectors doing the washing up. All of these activities are not exactly my idea of fun but they were for Harry and that's all that counts.

What I do know is that whatever Harry has planned for today I've got to purchase hair dye and colour my hair as per Harry's best man agreement. I want to do it before the rehearsal so Laura, Alice and co don't get too much of a shock on Saturday.

I just know that I'm going to look like a dickhead but because Harry has a weird hatred of grey hair I don't want to take any chances that he'll throw a tantrum on his wedding day if I don't do it. Does that sound absolutely ridiculous? Of course it does, but Harry does tend to look at life a little differently than most.

Ten minutes later Harry arrives downstairs.

'Why didn't you sleep longer? You've got a big day ahead of you.'

'Sleeping is wasting my time. Anyway, have you heard of Ringo Starr?'

'Of course. He was in the Beatles, they're the most famous band in the world.'

'Yeah I've heard about them. Ringo wrote *Octopus's Garden* and that's why they're so popular.'

I do think Lennon and McCartney also wrote a couple of tunes that seemed to have caught on.

'Ringo left those losers and became a fantastic actor. He should have won an Oscar for *Caveman*. He also narrated *Thomas The Tank Engine* videos from 1994 to 1996 and in America from 1989 to 1990. He's amazing and I want to meet him.'

OK, fair enough. Who wouldn't want to meet a Beatle?

'So we're going to Abbey Road studios today. It's about a ten minute walk from St John's Wood tube station. From Brixton we'll take the Victoria line to Green Park and change to the Jubilee line and it's three stops from there. I want to take photos of Ringo walking across that zebra crossing.'

'Harry, that was fifty odd years ago. I really don't think he'll be still be hanging around there.'

'He wore a black suit when he was walking across the road but he wasn't wearing a tie so why do I have to wear a tie on Saturday?'

'You have to wear a tie on your wedding day.'

'But you said that Ringo and those other geezers were the most famous band in the world but yet none of them worn any ties?'

'OK, Harry, can we drop this tie discussion please?'

Only Harry could try to argue that because Ringo and the 'other geezers' didn't wear a tie on a 1969 album cover this should justify why he shouldn't wear a tie on his wedding day.

'Harry, Ringo won't be at Abbey Road today, but if you want to go then we will.'

'He'll be there, so let's go.'

I have this image of Ringo Starr walking back and forth across that zebra crossing for the past fifty years.

'So are you getting nervous about the wedding?' I ask Harry.

'I don't know why I have to get married twice.'

'What do you mean?'

'Tonight and Saturday.'

'Tonight's just a rehearsal. It's like when you practice a song over and over again to make sure it's perfect.'

'So we have to go to that religious building over and over again to get married loads of times?'

'No, you just have to practice tonight what you're going to say on Saturday and where you're going to stand. The priest will explain everything.'

'But I'm going to miss *Family Fortunes* on UK Gold.'

'Just record it and watch it when we get back.'

'But it'll be too late cos that man in the black suit will be waffling on and on forever. Can't we just leave halfway through his chat?'

'The whole purpose of tonight is to help you and Bernadette prepare for your wedding day. You can't just leave in the middle of it.'

'But Les Dennis is the quiz master tonight. He's a genius and much funnier than Max Bygraves.'

'Are you telling me you watched Family Fortunes when Max Bygraves was in it?'

'Of course I do. The problem is the producers won't let Bygraves sing on that show, which is a disgrace cos I just love *You're A Pink Toothbrush*.'

I'm half expecting him to say that he's changed his mind and chosen that tune for their wedding song.

'What do you think about spending the weekends in Croydon with Bernadette?'

'Croydon is Monday, Tuesday, Wednesday, Thursday and Sunday nights. Friday and Saturday nights are in Streatham.'

'But you'll be with Bernadette at the weekends in Croydon, won't you?'

'No, Croydon is only Monday, Tuesday…'

'OK, I understand but after the wedding you'll be sleeping with Bernadette all the time, won't you?'

'I'm in this house on Friday and Saturday nights forever.'

'Oh I see, you want Bernadette to stay here at the weekends?'

'No, I'm sleeping in my Streatham bed on my own. I don't know where Bernadette will sleep.'

'Is she aware of this?'

Harry just shrugs his shoulders. 'Don't know, shall I ring her up and find out?'

I nod my reply.

I blame myself for this. I just assumed that after the wedding they would be staying together in Croydon. I never thought for a second that Harry wanted to continue with his weekend sleeping arrangements. It doesn't make any sense.

Although it's only four-thirty in the morning Harry rings Bernadette and she answers straight away. Sleeping is not a top priority in the autistic world.

'OK, I'll probably see you at six,' Harry says, referring to the rehearsal time, as he hangs up.

Probably?

'Yeah, she's not staying here at the weekends.'

'Why not?'

'She doesn't like the wallpaper in my bedroom.'

'But it's Thomas wallpaper?'

'She just hates wallpaper. It makes her nervous.'

I do remember Alice telling me this a while ago.

'Would she stay if I strip the wallpaper off?'

'No way are you getting rid of it. You put it up in 2001, so it brings back memories for me and I don't want you to destroy my memories.'

So Harry would rather keep the Thomas wallpaper in his bedroom than have Bernadette stay. When it's a decent hour I shall have to ring Alice to discuss this new development. Presumably she's also unaware of this?

'What about you staying at Bernadette's at weekends?'

'No way, Alice and that Greg bloke laugh too much. It gives me a headache and I don't want to see them with their mouths open all the time.'

'Harry, when you commit to getting married it's usually means staying with your wife all the time, not just during the week.'

'Is that a new rule?'

'It's not a rule as such, it's just what most people do.'

'Can you make me my Frosties, but without the milk?' He asks.

'Harry, I know that this is late in the day to be asking you this question, but do you still love Bernadette?'

'Of course, especially on Mondays, Tuesdays, Wednesdays, Thursdays and Sundays. Friday and Saturday are my days off.'

Days off from marriage?

I've had some strange conversations with Harry over the years but this one takes some beating. Bernadette doesn't want to stay with Harry because she doesn't like wallpaper and Harry doesn't want to stay at Alice and Greg's as he doesn't like to see their mouths when they're laughing.

As if I wasn't nervous already, now I'm increasingly worried about how committed they are to each other.

A few hours later Alice confirms that Bernadette will be staying at hers for the weekends. She didn't know anything about this until she asked her daughter whilst on the phone with me. She doesn't seem as bothered about it. She told me that Bernadette is extremely routine driven. Sleeping with Harry during the week is enough of a change that it'll do her good to stick to the weekend regime for the time being. Alice made some good points and I feel better after speaking to her.

We head out early and reach Abbey Road by eight o'clock. Being a big Beatles fan I've been here a few times previously and it's usually packed with tourists having their photos taken walking on the famous zebra crossing but today there is only an American couple.

'Excuse me, buddy, but you do mind taking our photo?' The man asks me.

'At last, an American. Are you friends with Tom Hanks?' Harry inquires.

'No, unfortunately not.'

'What about Jim Carrey?'

'I'm afraid I don't know anyone famous.'

'Let me see your smile.'

Understandably the man looks perplexed.

'My son's autistic.' The man immediately smiles at us both.

'I knew it. You're the best smiler I've ever seen. Nobody smiles in Streatham.'

I take the iPhone off the man and take several photos of the couple walking back and forth. A few cars beep their horns in annoyance at having to wait but if you're going to be driving this way you'll have to expect this. It's a no brainer.

'Shut the fuck up, you arseholes,' Harry shouts at them. 'Can't you see they're Americans?'

The couple leave soon after and we cross the road to look at the wall outside the Abbey Road studios as it's full of loving messages for the Fab Four. Harry takes out his felt tip pen and writes 'I love you, Ringo. Your narration on the *Thomas And The Breakdown* episode is spectacular.' Is mentioning Thomas on the Abbey Road wall a first?

Despite my mild protests we've been standing outside the studios for over an hour and during this time Harry has been anxiously looking left and right, almost as if he's watching a tennis match.

'Where the fuck is he?' Harry asks.

'Harry, Ringo's probably in America touring or recording. We've spent long enough here so let's go.'

But as soon as the words leave my mouth a big limousine pulls up in front of us and unbelievably Ringo Starr gets out.

'Hi guys,' he says.

'Why aren't you walking on the road? Are you fed up of doing that now?' Harry asks his hero.

'My son's autistic,' I explain.

'Can you sign my Thomas DVD covers please?'

Ringo hesitates but does sign all of them. I seem to remember that he doesn't do autographs anymore but I think mentioning Harry's autism swung it in our favour.

'What's your favourite Thomas episode?'

'It's so long ago I can't remember.'

'I've left one of my Thomas DVD covers at home but don't worry I can forge your signature. By the way do you want to be my best man?'

The ex-Beatle looks confused until I tell him that Harry is getting married on Saturday.

'I'm afraid I'm busy on Saturday but congratulations and I wish you the best of luck.'

'I'm now going to have *Octopus's Garden* as my wedding song.'

Not ideal, but an improvement on *Saturday Night's Alright For Fighting*, *Ernie (The Fastest Milkman In*

The West) and the outside contender *You're A Pink Toothbrush.*

We chat with Ringo for a few more minutes. He explained that he was there because they're filming a documentary on Abbey Road studios. Harry was just staring at him in awe and didn't say another word. He kindly posed for a photo before going into the studio. What a nice guy. I can honestly say I've never seen Harry so excited. We were lucky there was nobody else around so he probably felt more relaxed to chat.

We wait around for a passer-by to come along and with his help we get the famous zebra crossing photo done. Once again a few cars beep us but Harry isn't taking that lightly.

'If you don't fuck off I'll get my dad to beat the shit out of you.' Luckily none of the drivers take up Harry's offer.

'That was incredible, what were the odds on that happening?' I say, in disbelief at meeting a Beatle.

'Yeah, Archie was right, although he got the time wrong.'

'What are you talking about?'

'Archie Doncaster has a website called *Ringo is the best Thomas narrator.* He's a bit obsessed about Thomas.'

I don't believe that for one minute.

'Anyway he found out that Ringo was doing a documentary here cos he met him yesterday. He put it on his website last night. But he said that Ringo arrived at eight-thirty but today he came at thirteen minutes past nine. He probably had a lie in.'

'Hold on, so you knew that Ringo might be here today?'

'Yeah, that's right but I thought he'd be still walking on the road when we got here.'

'If people knew about it why are we the only ones here?'

'Because Archie's website only had two hits, me and some bloke in Uruguay.'

'But why didn't you tell me about this?'

'Because you don't like documentaries.'

That explains everything.

Even though I was a child I remember going to see the Beatles film *A Hard Days Night* with my father. I have this vivid image of people waiting in the queue wearing Beatles wigs. After leaving that cinema that day I became a Beatles fan for life. My mum hated them. She used to call them 'long haired louts' and 'everyone will forget they existed this time next year.' On that wonderful afternoon in 1964 I never for one second thought that I would meet a Beatle, especially via a *Thomas The Tank Engine* route.

On the way home we had the Ringo photo developed (one for Harry and one for me) and I purchased the dreaded hair dye.

Throughout the afternoon Harry is watching several Thomas DVDs while tightly clutching his Ringo photo and I dye my hair. I was right I look like a sad dickhead who is trying to relive his youth.

'That's much better, no more grey hairs on your head and in this house,' is Harry's assessment.

'Come on, Harry, it's time to go to the church.'

'But I'm going to miss *Family Fortunes*.'

'I told you just tape it.'

'But Les Dennis is much funnier when I'm watching it live.'

'It makes no difference.'

'Yes, it does.'

Twenty minutes later we arrive at the church. Laura, Alice, Sean, Greg and of course Bernadette are waiting for us. As we approach them Laura and Alice start laughing.

'What the hell did you do that for?' Laura asks as she's glancing at my jet black hair.

'All part of a gentleman's agreement with Harry.'

They look confused.

'Sorry, we're late. Harry was complaining about missing *Family Fortunes*.'

'Yeah, I got mum to tape it for me but it's just not the same,' Bernadette chips in.

We all enter the church and are immediately greeted by Father Quinlan.

'And how are we all today?' He asks.

'If you just cut out the claptrap and maybe we'll be able to see Les Dennis live,' Harry says.

Father Quinlan looks confused. I shake my head to indicate to him not to pursue this dialogue.

Ten minutes later just as Father Quinlan is explaining the meaning behind the vows Harry interrupts him.

'This is all bullshit. I've changed my mind. I don't want to get married.'

'Harry, it's important to listen to the priest. He won't take too much longer.'

Harry looks at Bernadette. 'Do you mind if I don't marry you on Saturday?'

Bernadette stares at him but doesn't respond.

'It was really nice of you to give me half of your Kit Kat but there's too much wedding crap going on and it's giving me a headache and the shits. We can do this in three years' time. Is that OK?'

'I want to marry you, Harry because you're a brilliant man and a great piano player, but I'll wait three years, that's no problem.'

'OK, thanks. Do you want to come to my house to watch Les Dennis?'

'Yes.'

'Hold on, Harry, are you serious about this?' I ask.

'I just told you, didn't I?'

'I remember feeling anxious just before I married your father. It's just nerves, that's all. You'll be OK so don't worry too much,' Laura tells her son.

'I don't care, I'm not getting married. Now I want to go home and watch *Family Fortunes*.'

I am stunned. I assumed that Harry was not taking any interest in the wedding build up. I had no idea that he was having second thoughts.

'It sounds like he really means it,' a clearly worried Alice tells me.

'Let me have another chat with him, just the two of us,' I say to the bewildered wedding party.

'Harry, follow me,' I command as I guide him out of the church.

'What do you want?' Harry asks.

'We have fifty-eight people coming to your wedding on Saturday, you can't just back out now.'

'I can.'

'There's about a dozen people coming over from Ireland.'

'Just give them that Guinness drink. That'll make them all happy.'

'But you saw the look on Bernadette's face. She was so disappointed. You've let her down.'

'I'll buy her a Flintstones DVD, that'll cheer her up.'

'Why are you so against marrying Bernadette?'

'I've been getting headaches about it for the last thirty-seven hours. I want to be with Bernadette but I don't want all those Guinness people and everyone else just staring at me and that man in black talking absolute gobshite.'

'If you want we can have a quieter wedding.'

'Bernadette said that it's OK to wait three years before we do it again.'

'Harry, she had no choice. Bernadette loves you and she'll wait for you. But what's going to be the difference in waiting that time? You can just do this on Saturday with just a few of us if you like?'

'No, I can't,' he replies with such a painful expression that just breaks my heart. I put my arms around him and start to cry. 'If that's what you want then it's OK,' I tell my son.

Bernadette rushes over to Harry, holds both his hands and kisses them. There are tears rolling down her cheeks.

'Don't worry, Harry. I understand. We'll do it all again in 2024.'

Harry smiles at her but he looks sad. I go back into the church and tell everyone that as far as I know the wedding is off but I'll confirm this later after I've had another chat with him at home. Laura looks so worried for her son and dashes out of the church to give him a hug. As usual his arms remain firmly by his side.

Harry and Bernadette get in my car and we drive home.

They both watch *Family Fortunes* in silence and after it's over I sit in the armchair opposite them.

'I'm still not clear why you don't want to get married?' I ask my son.

'My head has been exploding for thirty-seven hours. I know that I have autism and I don't know any other autistic person who's married, so I don't think it can be done.'

'Harry, there are plenty of autistic adults who are married, so don't worry about that.'

'But I've been feeling sickly whenever I think I'm going to be a married husband. I keep on shitting myself.'

'Bernadette, don't you think he'll make a great husband?'

'I won't know until we're married.'

Thanks for the backup.

'Well I think you'll make a fantastic husband. You've always been so kind and caring to Bernadette; hasn't he?' I look at Bernadette.

'Yes, apart from when he plays the Adam West Batman film.' She replies.

'Bernadette thinks you're a caring person, so that means you'll make a good husband.'

'There's going to be too many people in the church. I'll be falling over everyone.'

'I've told you all along there's going to be fifty-eight people and you didn't seem bothered. But as I said to you earlier if you just want me, your mother and Alice there, that'll be fine.'

'I'm going to be a shit married person. I just got too excited when Bernadette gave me half of her Kit Kat.'

Bernadette is wiping her tears away but still has her other arm around Harry. Even at this most distressing time she's still being so affectionate towards my son.

I feel like crying at the scene in front of me.

'It's OK, Harry, I understand. You're worried not only about the wedding itself but also if you're up to being a good husband. I'll cancel the wedding.'

He looks at me and smiles.

'But I still want to go to Halifax.'

Bernadette nods in agreement.

CHAPTER FORTY: 1994

'My name is Doctor Rickman. And how are you today, Harry?'

Harry just looks at the floor and doesn't respond.

'Are you going to answer the doctor?' I ask my son.

Harry's eye divert to the window.

'Is there anything out there that interests you?' Rickman inquires.

Harry just stares out of the window and doesn't respond.

'He's probably a bit nervous, so is it OK if I ask you some questions, David?'

'Of course, go ahead.'

'I understand your wife is recovering from a nervous breakdown. Is that correct?'

'Yes it is.'

'Can you give me some background to this?'

'Are you implying that because Laura had a nervous breakdown that she was always mentally unstable and consequently one of the reasons why Harry's having the problems he's got now?'

'I'm just trying to get a picture of your family's medical history. Not just Laura, but yourself, parents, brothers, sisters, uncles, aunts, cousins, etc. Please bear with me on this.'

'I'm sorry, I didn't mean to fly off the handle. It's a stressful time.'

'I perfectly understand.'

'Laura was always the strongest person in our relationship. Friends have told us that she was tougher than me, that's why I'm shocked to see how she is now.'

'My notes say that her illness was a result of the stress involved in dealing with Harry's behavioural issues. Is that right?'

'Yes, without a doubt. Since he was born Harry just wasn't a good sleeper. Two to three hours is his average and when he's up either Laura or me have to be up with him. I explained all of this to Carol.'

'Yes, we have it documented but I want to go over it again just in case there's something that was missed.'

'It wasn't just the sleep deprivation that put us both on edge, there were other issues. He's very aggressive and constantly hits Laura and me for no apparent reason. He does the same to the other kids in his nursery. He's now on his fourth nursery school as he's got chucked out of the other three and I'm guessing it's only a matter of time before he has to leave his current one.'

'That's really stressful for you both.'

'Yeah, you're not kidding. He went through a couple of years just smearing his excrement everywhere and was only toilet trained a couple of months ago. As you've already seen his communication skills are lacking, he doesn't make any eye contact and hasn't got much language. He's insular and doesn't have any friends. It was Laura who first raised the alarm bells. I just thought he was a bit slow and he'll catch up but she insisted that we saw a psychiatrist but it was during the period of seeing Carol that the lack of sleep and the stress of Harry's behaviour began to get on top of Laura. So instead of Carol's sessions helping us both, Laura got more edgy and anxious about everything. Our local doctor prescribed medication to calm her nerves and help her sleep, but it just made her listless and she just completely distanced herself from Harry and me. So much so that she insisted that we move out of the house as we were increasing her anxiety. She totally blames Harry for her illness. She's a changed person.'

Rickman is frantically writing down my comments.

'She's never had any mental health issues prior to this if that's any help to you?' I add.

'Does she know why you and Harry are here today?'

'No, I haven't discussed it with her. Although I feel bad about keeping this from her I just don't feel the time is right.'

'Thanks for sharing that information. Now do you mind giving me your medical history?'

'I have high blood pressure, but that's about it.'

'Do you take any medication for it?'

'Yes, a drug called Ramipril. I think it's a fairly low dosage but off the top of my head I can't recall what that is.'

'That's OK. Are your parents still alive?'

'No, they passed away many years ago.'

'What were the causes of death?'

'My father had lung cancer and my mother emphysema. Both were heavy smokers.'

'Did they have any mental health issues?'

'Although she didn't take anything for it I'd say that my mother suffered from depression.'

'In what way did that manifest itself?'

'She frequently had migraines and always seemed down and very moody. Her glass was always half empty.'

'Ok, what about Laura's parents?'

'They're no longer with us either, but as far as I know there were no medical issues. They died of old age a couple of years ago.'

Rickman looks over at Harry who is now standing still and staring out of the window.

'Are you OK there, Harry?' He asks.

Harry doesn't respond.

'He does that a lot,' I say.

'What do you mean?'

'Just not responding. I should get his hearing checked.'

'I'll talk about this later, but I just want to carry on with the medical history. Do you know of anyone in both families who has depression, bipolar, anxiety issues or schizophrenia?'

'There's a cousin of mine in Ireland that has bipolar. He's in his early fifties. As far as I know nobody else has those issues.'

'How bad is his bipolar? Does it require time off work? Does it affect his sleeping?'

'No, not really. His demeanour's very similar to my mum, he always looks a bit troubled.'

'Any language disorders in any of your relatives?'

'No.'

'What about ADHD?'

'Some of Laura's family are quite hyper, but they've never been diagnosed with ADHD. To be honest I didn't know much about it until Carol's diagnosis a few weeks ago.'

'I won't take too much longer on this, but I want to ask if there's a history of neurological disorders, like epilepsy, alzheimers, multiple sclerosis, parkinsons or brain tumours?'

'I really don't think so. Obviously Laura would know more about her family history.'

'One last question, are any of your family members a little slow, a bit behind their peers?'

'No.'

'OK, thanks for that.'

'So what does all that tell you?'

'Apart from Laura's breakdown and your mother's depression the family history looks OK. Do you look like your mother or father?'

'Definitely my mother. Everyone says that. My sister, Fiona, looks more like Dad.'

Again he writes all this down.

'Now I want to bring in a couple of consultants to run a few simple tests with Harry. Do you mind sitting at the back of the room? We just want his full attention. We might even ask you to leave the room, if that's OK?'

'I don't mind, whatever's best for you.'

The two consultants arrive and introduce themselves. Rickman asks Harry to sit opposite him which he does. For the next fifteen minutes they ask my son various questions about why he gets angry, his sleep patterns, his relationships with me, Laura, his teachers, fellow pupils etc. Harry either doesn't reply or just gives one word answers. At no point does he make eye contact with anyone. They give him simple physical tests like trying to match square, circle, rectangle objects into their relevant shapes and even from my distance I can see that he's struggling with that.

'Thank you, Harry for your time, you've been very helpful,' Rickman kindly tells my son.

Soon after they all leave the room, informing me they just want to discuss their findings and will return shortly.

I sit next to Harry and put my arm around him. He's engrossed in his Thomas book.

I wish that Laura was here with us. She should be. Why didn't I tell her about this? I didn't want to cause her any more anxiety and possibly cause a relapse. Amanda told me yesterday that she's starting to instigate conversations with her, which is a massive progression. It gives me a ray of hope that someday we'll all be back together again as a family.

Nearly an hour later the three consultants return and sit opposite me.

'David, we've studied all your comments and observed Harry for the past hour or so and I have to tell you that in our professional opinion Harry is on the autistic spectrum.'

I don't remember anything else Rickman says for the next few minutes. Although I'd been expecting this it still comes as a shock to hear those words. I can see his lips moving but I can't hear a sound.

'I'm so sorry to give you this news, I really am. Have you got any questions?'

'My mind just went blank. What are the reasons for your diagnosis?' I ask.

'Pretty much the same as Carol's. He's very insular, has no eye contact, very little speech, the smearing of the excrement over a long period of time, unwarranted aggression and extremely routine driven. He was unable to answer nearly all of our questions and couldn't perform the structured physical tests. You asked earlier about his hearing when I asked him a question but I think his lack of response is more to do with his social isolation. At this point I'm not sure if Harry has Aspergers or is more severely autistic. I consulted with my two colleagues and they're convinced that he has Aspergers, but without being the profit of doom I think it may be a little too early to come to that conclusion. I will get this all officially documented and notify your local surgery and the relevant education bodies. He needs to get into a special needs pre-school as soon as possible. Early intervention is vital.'

'This is a lot to take in.'

'I know and I just wish it could be better news for you.'

'What about Carol's ADHD diagnosis? Do you agree with that?'

'Yes, he most definitely has ADHD, OCD and ODD. Sufferers from OCD constantly feel high levels of anxiety and their ritualistic behaviours reduce these anxieties. However, generally they do not enjoy their routine compulsions and do feel an over-riding sense of urgency to perform these actions in case something bad happens. Within our report we'll be recommending the relevant medication. '

'But surely he's too young to start taking medicine?'

'I know it's hard to take in right now but believe me it'll help Harry.'

'As it was only a couple of weeks ago when Carol mentioned autism to me I'm not too clued up on it, but am I right in saying that there's no cure?'

'Yes, that's correct. It's a life-long condition, but with behavioural techniques and the right medication it is manageable. I know that this is distressing and worrying news but please do not despair.'

'I want McDonalds,' Harry proclaims, as we get into the hospital lift.

He obviously has no idea of the implications of his hospital visit. At no point has he asked me why we're here.

I look at my son and wonder what life has in store for him. It's certainly going to be very different to the one that Laura and myself had envisaged. I've no idea what to do from this point onwards regarding his education, but I'm sure in time it'll all become clearer. I've got a lot of catching up to do on the subject of autism.

As we approach the hospital front entrance I'm stunned to see Laura and Amanda at the reception desk.

'I've already told you I'm Harry McCarthy's mother and I want to see my son *now*,' Laura shouts at a harassed looking receptionist.

'Laura, what are you doing here?'

'When the fuck where you going to tell me about this appointment?' She asks.

Amanda is standing behind Laura and the penny drops how my wife found out.

'I didn't want to cause you any more anxiety. I was trying to protect you.'

'Harry's my son as well. I've a right to know what the fuck is going on.'

I'm not sure if Laura's aggressive tone is a good or bad sign. In the early stages of her illness she was often angry and edgy but once the medicine kicked in she completely zoned out, so I haven't seen her like this for a couple of months.

'A couple of weeks ago Carol was pretty sure that Harry was autistic,' I say.

'What the fuck does she know?'

'Well he is.'

'Who says so?'

'I've just had an appointment with three autism consultants. They asked me loads of questions on our families' medical histories and the whole background on Harry. They also gave Harry some structured tests and had a chat with him. Despite your reservations about Carol she was actually spot on with her diagnosis. These consultants are amongst the best in the country and they have no doubt that Harry is autistic.'

Laura just stares at me, shaking her head.

'That just can't be true.'

'It's one hundred percent true,' I reply, as I attempt to hug her but she recoils from me.

'Laura, let's go outside for a walk,' Amanda says.

Laura glances at her sister and slowly walks alongside her. She continues to shake her head and just stares at the ground as she's walking. She's holding onto Amanda's arm for support. She looks so weak but Amanda appears calm and confident in her new role as carer. She's obviously been dealing with her in this physical and mental state a lot in the past few weeks.

After walking around in complete silence for half an hour Amanda hails a cab.

'Do you want us to share it with you?' I ask.

'Best not,' Amanda replies.

Amanda helps Laura into the taxi. As it pulls away Amanda gives us a half smile but Laura doesn't look in our direction.

Not once did Laura say anything to her son.

CHAPTER FORTY-ONE

'Harry, it's natural to feel nervous about the wedding. Your mother told you yesterday that she was anxious before she married me. Lots of people feel this way.'

'Yeah and mum fucked off when I was a boy. She shouldn't have got married either.'

'We were both very happy together but then she fell ill.'

'Was she ill because she was married?'

'No, it just happened.'

I'll never tell Harry the real reason behind Laura's breakdown.

'Bernadette was so disappointed yesterday.'

'Did you order that Flintstones DVD on Amazon?'

'Not yet, but a Flintstones DVD isn't going to make her feel better right now. She loves you and wants to marry you.'

I'm walking a fine line here. I honestly believe that Harry wants to get married but he's scared. Although I don't want to pressurise him I need to know for certain one way or another as there's fifty-eight guests to contact if he stands by his decision.

He's holding his Thomas book and just staring at the front cover. It's his safety blanket.

'What's the reason why you don't want to get married?' I ask Harry again.

'I feel frightened like I did when I watched that film where the shark ate all those people.'

'Do you mean *Jaws*?'

'Yes, I kept on having dreams that the shark was following me when I went shopping in Streatham and then he ate me for his dinner.'

'OK, I'm going to ask you one last time, do you want me to cancel the wedding?'

'Yes, now can you give me my Frosties but don't put any milk on them, I don't like it when they're soggy.'

'Harry, I do understand your anxieties and I'll do whatever you want,' I say to my son.

'I'm hungry. Where's my Frosties?'

I contact Alice and let her know Harry's final decision. Considering it was her daughter that had been jilted hours before the wedding she's amazingly understanding. I have found that the parents of autistic children that I know definitely have an affinity with each other. We're all dealing with similar issues that most 'normal' parents never encounter. There's a special bond between us all and Alice is a prime example of this. She's had a tough life. Her husband Francis left when Bernadette was four, leaving Alice to bring up her daughter on her own. I don't for a second underestimate the problems a 'normal' single parent has to encounter but you have to multiply that many times over when you're raising a special needs child. Although Alice is understandably disappointed, she's taken it all on board and even asked after Harry's well-being.

Alice tells me that Bernadette is still keen to go to Halifax so we arrange to meet up on Sunday for our break with the 'not so newlyweds.' Luckily, I didn't book the honeymoon suite at the hotel.

The first person I contact is Laura.

'He hasn't changed his mind,' I immediately say to her. There's no room for small talk right now.

'I didn't think he would.'

'I really feel for Bernadette. She looked so sad but was doing her best to hide it. She showed great maturity.'

'Absolutely. She couldn't stop hugging him.'

'That was hard to watch,' I say.

'Did he mention anything about rescheduling it?'

'No. Yesterday he said he'll marry in three years' time but I just think it's a Harryism. I've no idea what the future holds for them both.'

'Was it just nerves?'

'Yeah I think so. He must've been bottling it up because I had no idea how worried he was about it. In fact I thought that he wasn't taking it all seriously.'

'Do you want me to ring the guests?'

'Nah, don't worry, I'll take care of that.'

'David, I was going to tell you last night but we've made a decision about the Ireland move.'

'Well, don't keep me waiting.'

'We're going for it. Sean's contacted the Irish estate agent and put in an offer that was accepted straight away. He's already put his house on the market.'

'Wow, that's happened quickly.'

'There's no chain on the Irish end and Sean's willing to accept a slightly lower price on his place, so I think we'll be moving sooner rather than later, if it all goes according to plan.'

'And what's happening with your Streatham flat?'

'The current rental lease runs out in ten weeks and I've already given notice to the tenants so it's going to be my UK base.'

'Sean must be delighted.'

'He's absolutely thrilled to bits. It's lovely to see him so happy.'

'And what about you?'

'I know it's going to be a big adjustment for me but I think it's the right time for the move. I just hope that Harry's more settled before I go.'

'He's going to be just fine. His state of mind is no different from most other prospective grooms. I give him a lot of credit for making that decision. That was brave. I really believe that it will all come good in the end, so don't worry about him.'

I was both pleased and a little sad to hear Laura's news about the Ireland move. However I honestly believe that she'll be happy there and it'll give me a good excuse to visit.

The next person I contact is Father Quinlan. As it all kicked off in front of him only yesterday he wasn't surprised to receive my call and hear the news. He told me that if Harry ever changed his mind in the coming weeks he would make himself available as soon as possible. That was reassuring especially as his Saturday overtime had just gone down the swanny.

Although the Irish contingent hadn't boarded their flights, nearly all of them are still making a trip over to make a weekend of it, which makes me feel better. Half a dozen of them plan to visit the Emirates stadium to try and purchase some tickets for the Arsenal game off the touts.

It takes most of the morning to contact all the guests and go through that painful conversation over and over again.

Harry meanwhile is settled in front of the TV watching cartoon network. As far as I know he hasn't contacted Bernadette.

How can a day that started off by meeting Ringo Starr end so dismally? I wonder if Ringo had accepted Harry's best man invitation would the wedding still be going ahead?

I dyed my hair shortly before leaving for the church yesterday. I wish I had waited. I look like a sad middle aged man who is desperately trying to recapture his youth. I am hoping that some grey hairs reappear before I return to work, although to be honest, I could go to work just wearing speedos and flip flops and my IT colleagues wouldn't notice.

I've also got to contact Harry's home as they have already reallocated Harry and Bernadette's old rooms and redecorated their new room. I also have to speak to Social Services to keep them updated on the latest developments.

I get a can of beer out of the fridge and venture out to the garden. It's a beautiful afternoon and the weather forecast for tomorrow is hot and sunny, the perfect day to get married. So what should I do tomorrow instead of seeing my son getting married? I was half thinking about meeting up with my Irish cousins for the Arsenal game but Harry wouldn't enjoy that and whatever I do I want to spend the day with my son.

It's quiet out here in my small South London garden. As I sip my beer I reflect on the changing circumstances of the people that I am closest to. Laura will be moving to Ireland in the coming months; Kerry will expedite the divorce proceedings and Harry now faces an uncertain future with Bernadette. A lot of changes.

I haven't contacted Kerry about the wedding cancellation but I'm not really up to having that conversation right now. I'll text her when I'm in Halifax.

And what about the Halifax trip? I was looking forward to spending time with the newlyweds and seeing how they were coping with their new status, but now it'll feel strange. However, Harry and Bernadette are keen to go. I hope it'll build bridges between them.

Harry wanders into the garden holding his ever present Thomas books and Ringo Starr photo.

'Have you spoken to Bernadette today?' I ask.

'No.'

'Don't you think you should? You did hurt her feelings yesterday, remember?'

'She's fine. Anyway, it's twelve minutes past four on a Friday and I never speak to her on Friday evenings.'

'You should make an exception for today.'

'No, rules are rules.'

'Have you thought anymore about when you want to get married again?'

'Yes, Saturday November the twenty-third, two thousand and twenty-four.'

'Does Bernadette know about this date?'

'No, but I'll text her tomorrow.'

I'm sure Mister Darcy would have done exactly the same if the technology was available in his day.

'Do you feel better now we've cancelled the wedding?'

'My headache has disappeared and I don't feel like shitting myself anymore.'

'So have you thought about what you want to do tomorrow?'

'I don't want to do anything. I just want to stay in Streatham, even though it's a shithole.'

'But you always want to go somewhere, so why don't we go into London? We could go to a gig or to the theatre.'

'Are any of the BBC weather forecasters in the theatre plays?'

'I don't think so.'

'Then it's a waste of time. I love it when they tell me it's going to piss down with rain.'

'What about going to see *The Lion King*? You liked the film.'

'Nah, I don't like hairy blokes and birds playing lions, that's just repulsive.'

'There's a Queen exhibition on in South Kensington. That's the pop group not Her Majesty.'

'The Queen has a lovely voice. I bet she's a great singer. Has she made any albums?'

'Not that I'm aware of.'

'I like the Queen group but I didn't like it when that Freddie bloke told his mother that he killed someone. Why did he do that?'

'Harry, that's just fiction. He didn't really kill anyone.'

'But he said in Bohemian Rhapsody that he shot some bloke in the head and he was boasting about it. And whenever he sang that song everyone clapped him. If I shot someone would everyone clap me?'

'It's just made up. It didn't happen.'

'Well he kept banging on about it for years. No, I don't want to see the Queen murderers.'

'What about going back to the Streatham bus stop and note down the latest bus timings?' I ask.

'Nah, that inspector was a fucking simpleton. I've already sent my spreadsheet to the London Transport head office and I'm just waiting for their reply.'

I wouldn't normally suggest such an outing as it wasn't exactly the most stimulating afternoon I've ever had but I'm desperate for some activity tomorrow to take my mind off what was originally planned.

'Can you buy me a piano tomorrow?' Harry asks.

'What's the matter with your keyboard?'

'It's crap. That Liberace bloke would never play a keyboard so why should I?'

'OK, that sounds like a good idea.'

I have been meaning to buy Harry a piano for ages and we do have enough space in the living-room so I think it'll give us both a much needed lift to get one.

'There's a good music shop in Streatham; we can have a look in there,' I say.

'No way, all the shop people in there are cross-eyed. There's some great piano shops in Tottenham Court Road. The only problem is how are we going to carry it onto the tube?'

That's a bit of a coincidence that all the staff are cross-eyed.

'The shop will deliver it to our house.'

'I knew that the Tottenham Court Road shop is better.'

'But didn't you say that you wanted to stay in Streatham?'

'I've changed my mind cos we don't have to carry the piano now.'

'I thought you hate it when someone changes their mind?'

'Oh yes, it makes my head go all fuzzy, even when I do it. Can we put the piano in the garden so I can give open air concerts at the weekend?'

'No, it's going in the living-room. Now do you want Bernadette to come along?'

'She can't, it's a Saturday.'

I forgot about Harry's weekend rules. I was going to mention that he would have broken the rules for his wedding day but it's best to stay clear of that subject matter for now.

Harry returns to the house while I stay in the garden thinking about tomorrow and what would have been the happiest day of my life.

CHAPTER FORTY-TWO: 1994

'Happy birthday, Harry,' I say as I hand him his presents, which include the inevitable *Thomas The Tank Engine* videos, clothes and numerous toys.

Although I had bought his presents a while ago I still went shopping yesterday and purchased even more gifts. I want this to be his best birthday ever. I just feel so sorry for my son over the autism diagnosis.

His life is changed forever and at this very early stage I have no idea what direction it will take. The sessions with Carol will now wind down although I do have a meeting with her next week. I just need to know in more detail how I can manage his behaviour to make all of our lives easier.

Carol's unofficial diagnosis was hard to comprehend but it was shocking to hear Doctor Rickman confirm this. I will remember that moment for the rest of my life. How could I not?

I haven't inquired about any special needs pre-school; maybe I'm still in denial? But it's something I've got to address as soon as possible.

Harry is completely oblivious to everything. On the way home all he seemed interested in was finding somewhere to eat. He never questioned anything about our hospital visit.

I haven't heard anything from Laura since our hospital encounter. Amanda told me she's gone into her shell again and barely left her bedroom.

Laura always made a big fuss over Harry's birthdays. Last year we had a birthday party, which admittedly was only attended by family as his nursery school peers were too scared to come along. Today it's just Harry and me. I don't expect Laura to bring over a present, which says it all about her current state of mind.

'What do you want to do today?' I ask.

'Line up my Thomas videos.'

He must have close to twenty Thomas videos and when he wakes up he brings them all downstairs in his Thomas box and painstakingly lines them up on the living-room floor. This takes ages as he studies them from several different angles to ensure that they are perfectly in a straight row.

'You do that every morning. Do you want to go to a restaurant?'

'Yes.'

'What restaurant do you want to go to?'

'The food ones.'

'What about McDonalds?'

'Yes.'

I have no idea how a 'normal' four-year-old interacts with his father. Are they old enough to ask for designer clothes or the most expensive trainers? I wouldn't think so but I now realise that I'm completely in the dark on how young kids act and behave.

After his breakfast Harry excitingly opens his video and toy presents but doesn't touch the clothes presents.

He then rushes into the living-room to play his new acquired videos but not before lining them all up again.

His joy at opening his presents is captured on video. One day Laura will hopefully see her son's happy moment, but not today.

CHAPTER FORTY-THREE

Soon after I wake up I notice that there's a message on my mobile. 'Good luck for today. I'll be thinking of you and Harry.' It was from Kerry.

I don't respond as I really don't want to be having that conversation right now, albeit by text.

Although it's just before five o'clock, Harry is already up. He's nearly always up before me. He's usually in the living-room with his stack of DVDs piled up on the coffee table which he carries down from his bedroom every morning.

'Morning, Harry.'

As usual he doesn't respond.

'Breakfast?' I ask.

'Frosties, but without the milk.'

'I know it's a Saturday but why don't you ask Bernadette to come with us today? She loves your piano playing and she'd be excited to come along.'

'I can't, it's a Saturday.'

'Why don't you just break your rules for one day? She's feeling down at the moment, it'll cheer her up.'

'It's impossible.'

I've got used to Harry's pretzel logic over the years but sometimes it still leaves me baffled. I could have said to him that Bernadette's heart is broken because he cancelled the wedding but I wanted to play it down.

Harry's Saturday routine still overrides any empathy he may be feeling towards Bernadette.

Just before we head out of the house Laura rings me.

'How's Harry?' She asks.

'He's acting no different from any other day but as we know he keeps a lot hidden away from us. I'm getting a piano for him today, it's long overdue. He seems pleased about it.'

'Wow, who wouldn't be?'

'How are you feeling?'

'Deflated.'

'Me too.'

'But I do have some news. A couple came around to the house yesterday and this morning they've put in an offer. They're first time buyers so no chain. From what the estate agent told us the guy's parents are well off so it sounds like they've been given a helping hand. It's looking promising.'

'That's great news. I'm happy for you both.'

'Thanks, David. Sean's thrilled but I can't feel the same right now because of Harry.'

'Do you know roughly when it's all a done deal?'

'Apparently within a couple of months.'

I still can't believe that in a matter of weeks Laura will be living in Ireland. Whenever we spoke about it I tried to adopt a positive attitude and I do honestly believe that it's a good move but I'm going to miss her terribly. In the past couple of years it was only Laura that I confided in about my problems. Nobody else. The stressful and bitter relationship that we had for such a long time has disappeared in recent years.

A short time later we're on the train, London bound.

'Do you like Liberace?' Harry asks the passenger opposite him.

'The piano player?'

'Yes. He was just fantastic.'

'Don't know too much about him. A bit before my time.'

'He was born on May the sixteenth, nineteen-nineteen and snuffed it on February the fourth, nineteen eighty-seven. He was always smiling when he played but I never do that cos when I sit on the piano stool it hurts my arse.'

Understandably the man looks perplexed. That's my cue.

'I'm sorry, my son's autistic.'

He acknowledges me with a smile.

'We're going to get a piano today but I don't want a Liberace one cos that dazzles and makes my eyes go cross-eyed.'

So that's why all the staff in the Streatham piano shop are cross-eyed.

'And I'll tell the Tottenham Court Road staff that I don't want any Liberace glittery suits. I just wear a Thomas tee-shirt and jeans when I play.'

'OK, Harry. I think you've discussed in great detail your piano preferences, as well as Liberace's. Leave the man be.'

Harry is the first person to leave our train carriage at Victoria station. He dashes to the front of the train presumably in search of the driver. By the time I catch up with him he's already in deep conversation with the driver.

'Whenever someone jumps over the level crossing barrier when you're driving through do you run them over just to teach them a lesson for disobeying the railway's rules?' Harry asks.

'No, I'll try to stop but it's not always easy when I'm travelling at speed.'

'When you arrive at the station do you wave at all the passengers on the platform?'

'No, I'm focusing on stopping the train.'

'Good, cos they don't deserve that. They're all pricks, aren't they?'

The driver smiles at Harry and for once I don't have to dig out my 'I'm sorry, my son's autistic' catchphrase. He has enough sense to realise that Harry is special needs. You'll be surprised how many members of the public don't pick up on that.

'You must love it that you get to see all the South London towns every day and just drive through them cos they're all crapholes.'

The driver laughs at Harry's remark.

'OK, Harry, let's go now.'

'Hold on, aren't you forgetting something? Give the driver a twenty cos he was even better than the one we had last week.'

I know it's pointless to argue so I hand the driver a twenty pound note.

'What's that for?' He asks.

'For getting us to Victoria without any crashes. You're the dog's bollocks,' Harry proclaims.

'Please take it,' I add.

'That's the first tip I've ever had in twenty-six years as a driver; thanks so much,' he tells us as he walks away staring at his twenty pound note as if he'd just won the lottery.

'Well, Harry you've made one train driver very happy.'

'It was nothing.'

Yeah for you it was.

Half an hour later we arrive at the music shop.

'What pianos have you got?' Harry asks a salesman.

'Are you talking Grand, Upright or Electronic pianos?'

'Stop talking bullshit and show me a piano that's got white and black pieces and isn't glittering.'

'Sorry about that, my son's autistic. We just want one that'll fit into a living-room.'

Making sure that the piano fits into a living-room is surely enough of a specification for him to pinpoint the exact piano required?

Harry sits down at the first piano that he sees. He starts playing and singing *White Christmas* which is slightly out of place in the middle of August but this doesn't seem to bother a number of customers who stop to listen. When he finishes he gets a round a warm round of applause.

'Do you like this piano, sir?' The salesman asks.

'Ladies and Gentleman, I'll like to play my wedding song. I was supposed to get married in eighty-seven minutes time but the thought of it makes me sick to my stomach,' Harry announces, ignoring the salesman's question.

The 'audience' laugh, obviously thinking it's a joke. It isn't.

Harry then launches into *Saturday Night's Alright For Fighting*. He even stands up, still playing the piano while singing the chorus, encouraging the customers to sing along, which most of them do. He's gathering quite a crowd now. Some people are viewing his performance from the shop window while a few more who look like they were walking past the shop decide to pop in upon hearing the music. When he finishes the place erupts. Harry bows in response.

'Well sir, is this piano suitable for you?' The salesman asks again.

'Yes, it's got all the white and black pieces in the correct order, so I'll have it.'

The salesman informs me that it's on sale for nine hundred and ninety-nine pounds, which is actually slightly cheaper than I had anticipated, so I hand the man my bank card.

'It was a pleasure doing business with you,' the salesman tells us as we're leaving the shop.

'Just make sure those white and black pieces don't fall off when you carry it on the train.'

The salesman smiles at Harry.

'I'm so pleased that you haven't caught the cross-eyed disease,' Harry adds.

I manage to capture most of *White Christmas* on my iPhone and all of *Saturday Night*, so I'll send them across to Laura. However the fact that he mentioned the time of his wedding indicates that it's on his mind. Although I haven't discussed his wedding today I did try several times yesterday but his only response was to inform me to order plenty of pork pies for two thousand and twenty-four.

'Are you happy about getting a piano?' I ask my son.

'Well they didn't have any yellow or orange ones so I suppose black is OK. I didn't want that white one cos everyone would've written graffiti messages on it.'

As the piano will be in our living-room and therefore mostly seen by only myself and Harry I'm not sure how anyone could scrawl messages on it but I'm happy that Harry is satisfied with his choice.

Whenever I give Harry presents he never voluntarily says thank you. Sometimes either myself or Laura will prompt him to say thank you just to teach him manners and only then will he quietly utter those two words. I've just spent a thousand pounds on him but so far he hasn't expressed his gratitude, and I'm not going to ask for it. Another autistic trait.

'I thought you said that you wanted *Octopus's Garden* as your wedding song,' I say.

'Yeah I do, but I don't know how to play that song on the piano so I lied to my audience.'

'So what do you want to do now?' I ask my son.

'Can you go on a boat in the London river?'

'Yes, that's a great idea.' To be honest I'll agree to anything right now just to keep us both busy.

We head straight to Westminster Pier on the River Thames and wait only a few minutes for the next boat to arrive.

The tour guide addresses all the tourists on board.

'On your right is the most famous clock in the world, Big Ben. It was completed on the thirty-first of May eighteen fifty-nine. From the ground level to the belfry is three hundred and thirty-four steps and its height is…'

'Stop talking bullshit and let me know where I can pick up my swimming trunks,' Harry shouts at the tour guide. All the tourists turn around to locate the source of the interruption.

'I'm sorry, I don't understand?'

'When are we going swimming?'

'We're not. You can't swim in the Thames without prior permission from the Port of London Authority.'

'Harry, this is just a boat ride to see all the sights of London. We're not going swimming,' I tell my son.

'So we're on this boat just looking at shitty buildings that tell the time?'

'They're historical buildings,' I add.

'So that fraud man tricked us?' Harry says, pointing at the tour guide.

'No, he didn't. He never said anything about swimming, it's just a boat ride.'

'He's wasting my time.'

I look up and the rest of the passengers are still staring at us.

'Sorry for the interruption, please carry on,' I tell the tour guide.

Fifteen minutes we depart at the London Eye pier. We did get some dirty looks from some of the passengers who presumably wanted to hear historical facts on Big Ben, the Houses Of Parliament and the London Eye, but instead had to listen to Harry questioning the whereabouts of his swimming trunks, etc.

Purchasing a piano, Harry's impromptu gig and the swimming trunks outburst is enough excitement for an afternoon so we make our way home.

Upon our return Alice rings.

'How's Harry?' She asks.

'He seems OK. What about Bernadette?'

'She's spending a lot more time in her bedroom. She's quieter, but overall not too bad.'

'I'm so sorry about all of this. I just feel so bad for Bernadette.'

'David, please don't worry. It wasn't meant to be today but I feel sure they'll get married when the time is right.'

'Thanks for being so understanding.'

'David, Greg won't be coming with us tomorrow. He has to go to Zurich for a few days but he'll try to hook up with us mid-week.'

'That's a shame but hopefully we'll see him at some point in sunny Halifax.'

I had a nervous feeling from the moment I woke up today but hearing Alice's positive attitude has cheered me up and given me fresh hope.

Harry is asleep by nine o'clock, which is rare. Has his nervous exhaustion caught up with him? I wish more than anything that we can have a good father and son chat so I can try and get to the root of his problems. Unfortunately that's almost impossible.

I take a can of beer out of the fridge and venture out to the garden. Six months ago I couldn't believe it when Harry told me about his engagement. As the wedding day was approaching I was getting increasingly nervous. Was Harry taking the wedding seriously? Well it transpires he was. So much so that he cancelled what should have been the happiest day of his life.

I have no doubt that Harry and Bernadette love each other deeply and because of this I'm so disappointed that they didn't marry. However, I hope with all my heart it won't be long before Bernadette can run down the church aisle.

CHAPTER FORTY-FOUR: 1994

Although this is my house I knock on the front door.

'You've got a key,' Amanda says as she lets us in.

'I know but somehow it doesn't feel right. How is she?'

'Nervous.'

Laura is sitting in the armchair in the living-room. She glances up as Harry and I sit on the sofa opposite her.

'Do you want a drink?' Amanda asks.

'I'll have a beer if you've got one. Harry will have a coke.'

'No problem,' Amanda replies with a smile.

I am eternally grateful to Amanda. She was originally only going to stay for a month but as Laura's recovery was slow her employer kindly let her take as much time as required to look after her sister. And she's getting paid for it. Amanda and her employer have come to my rescue in the most stressful period of my life.

Amanda and Laura have always got on and it's obvious that Amanda is deeply concerned for her sister's well-being. She is a kind and caring person. These attributes have been invaluable in handling Laura's illness.

'How are you keeping?' I ask my wife.

'I feel shit every day.'

'Are you taking the prescribed medicines?'

'Oh yes, for what good they do.'

'When was the last time you saw a doctor?'

'Last Thursday.'

'And what did he say?'

'Keep taking the medicine.'

'He must've said more than that.'

'He told her to exercise more, take up a hobby and not lay in bed all day,' Amanda responds while handing us our drinks.

'But what's the point? I'm never going to get better,' Laura adds.

'I know it's not easy but you've got to make an effort to get healthy again.'

'What for?'

'For the two people sitting in front of you right now.'

Laura looks to the floor.

'You haven't spoken to Harry yet? You haven't even acknowledged his existence. It's been over eight weeks since you last saw him.'

Laura is still staring at the carpet.

'So you're not going to talk to him?'

I feel bad talking about my son as if he's somewhere else rather than sitting next to me.

'I want to come back here,' Harry blurts out.

'You can't,' Laura quickly replies.

'Why?'

'Because I don't want you to.'

'Laura, calm down,' I say.

'No, I'm not fucking calming down. I'm ill because of him and I just can't handle having either of you anywhere near me.'

I'm shocked at her bitter attack on us both. I hoped that after two months I would see some recovery. I was wrong.

'I don't care what *you* thought caused your illness but I do care how you speak to Harry. To openly accuse your son is just disgraceful. That's the second time you've done that,' I shout back at her.

'He fucking needs to know the truth.'

'Laura do you mind not swearing in front of Harry?' I say.

'He doesn't understand what I'm banging on about anyway,' Laura replies with a bitter edge to her voice.

'Don't you dare say such cruel things to Harry again. Do you hear me?' I shout at her. 'I've had enough of this, come on, Harry, let's go.'

I take my son's hand and leave what used to be my house.

I'm still fuming by the time I arrive 'home'. I do understand that she's had a very serious mental illness but the hostility that she still has towards us is hard to comprehend. Her mood swings are frightening. One minute she's staring at the floor seemingly afraid to speak and then she suddenly explodes.

Harry didn't speak throughout the short journey back.

'Are you OK?' I ask my son.

'What did I do wrong?'

'You've done nothing wrong. Mummy's not well right now and is confused but she'll get better. She didn't mean what she said.'

'OK, can I watch my *Tom and Jerry* video now?'

'Yeah, go ahead.'

The woman that we just visited looks exactly like my wife but she's a completely different person.

CHAPTER FORTY-FIVE

'Look, it's a Halifax WH Smiths. Can we go in to see what it's like inside?' Bernadette asks.

'Of course,' Alice replies.

Harry and Bernadette literally run into WH Smiths followed at a slower pace by myself, Laura and Alice. As expected it looks exactly the same as the Streatham store. Harry and Bernadette head straight to the children's book section. Every time I go into a book store with Harry I'm usually sitting on a chair suitable for a four-year-old while Harry looks at loads of books. I do get some strange looks from young parents as they watch a sixty-year-old man and his twenty-nine-year-old son hanging out in the kids' section.

After only five minutes Harry and Bernadette return.

'This store is fucking useless. They don't have any Thomas books. Let's go home now,' Harry demands.

'We're not going anywhere. We've just arrived.'

'But this Halifax town is absolute shit now.'

I thought the whole point of coming here was because Halifax was voted one of the worst cities in England. Is it better than Paris, Rome or New York? No, but it's actually quite a nice city. I like the fact that the first book store we visited is a Thomas free zone.

'There's a Waterstones just down the road so let's have a look in there,' I tell Harry.

Half an hour later we leave Waterstones with Harry and Bernadette both clutching two new Thomas books.

'Halifax is amazing. I want to live here but only if they tear down the WH Smiths,' Harry announces.

Fickle.

'So now we've hit the only two book stores in town what else is there to do?' Laura asks.

'I want to be alone with Bernadette without all the old people following us,' Harry says while pointing at us.

I turn to Laura and Alice.

'We can all go for a coffee and leave them at a table on their own. I don't want them wandering around unaccompanied.'

'Absolutely agree,' Alice replies.

We head to the nearest Costa and while the three of us are having our cappuccinos, Harry and Bernadette are in deep conversation a few tables away. They could be either talking about rebuilding their relationship or discussing the storylines in the newly-acquired Thomas books.

'We think we've fucked up with the wedding so we want to set a new wedding date. It's going to be Saturday October the twenty-eighth two thousand and twenty-three.'

That extremely brief moment of excitement soon evaporated.

'So Dad, can you let the pork pie cooks know about the new date?'

'OK will do,' I reply.

'Well at least that's been brought forward thirteen months. We're getting there,' Laura says.

'Bernadette's so patient with Harry. What other jilted bride would react in the same way?' I ask. 'I'm sorry, Alice, I didn't mean to be so blunt.'

'Please, there's no need to apologise over that. Bernadette's doing OK. She told me yesterday that she really loves Harry and will just wait for him. Don't get too down about it all, it'll happen. Anyway, you've got enough on your plate right now.'

'Presumably you're referring to Kerry?'

'Yeah, any more news? If you don't mind me asking?'

'She texted me yesterday to wish us the best of luck but I didn't get back to her.'

It's a subject that I find too painful to talk about.

'Is she still going ahead with the divorce proceedings?'

'Yes, and as soon as I get back home I'll have to do the same. Something to look forward to.'

An awkward silence follows. I think that Alice has picked up the fact that I don't want to discuss it any further.

'Anyway, Harry, what about going to a museum this afternoon? There's quite a few to choose from. The Bankfield museum has a World War Two exhibition on. You enjoyed that Tom Hanks film *Saving Private Ryan* didn't you?' I ask, in a pathetic attempt to lure Harry into a museum.

'Museums are for boring old farts with no hair.'

Do I fall into that category?

'OK, so what do you want to do?' I ask with some trepidation.

'Harry, can we buy the Halifax Kit Kats in Sainsburys, Tesco, Waitrose, Marks & Spencer, Aldi and Poundland? We can give them marks out of ten and when we get back to Streatham we'll do it all over again and compare the results. The only condition is that we'll have to eat them straight away to get the full supermarket favour. We can't refrigerate them,' Bernadette proclaims.

'You're a genius. This is going to be my favourite honeymoon ever.'

Oh well, that's the rest of the day accounted for.

'Actually, David, I wouldn't mind doing a bit of shopping this afternoon. Do you mind?' Laura asks.

'Can I join you?' Alice chips in before I have a chance to reply.

'OK, on one condition, if they plan a similar outing tomorrow you'll both be in charge while I'll slip off to the pub. Agree?'

'Agreed,' they say at the same time and within a few minutes they disappear into the shopping mall.

We make our way to Sainsburys and straight to the confectionary aisle. Bernadette picks up a Kit Kat and heads straight for the checkout.

'Don't you want anything else?' I ask.

'No, it's only kit-kats that we're testing,' Bernadette replies, as she pays for it out of her own money.

'Harry, why don't you offer to pay for the Kit Kat?' I say.

'I can't, it's her favourite chocolate.'

It's that Harry logic again. They stop as soon as they leave the store and Bernadette breaks the Kit Kat in half and hands it to Harry, who nods and smiles at his fiancée.

After they devour their Kit Kats they have a five minute discussion to determine the markings. They jointly decide to give it a seven point six. I'm in charge of noting it all down on the Sainsburys receipt.

'This is so exciting,' Harry proclaims as they march off to the next supermarket.

I find this all ironic as it was a Kit Kat that Bernadette gave to Harry that prompted Harry's proposal.

For the next hour or so we visit all of the supermarkets required and the ratings varied from four point seven to nine point two and the winner is Waitrose. I'm still not sure how there can be such a variation in the markings but what I do know is that they've both eaten the equivalent of three Halifax Kit Kats.

'That was amazing. I want to spend all my summer holidays in Halifax now,' Harry announces.

'Me too, can I come with you?' Bernadette asks.

'Of course, we'll always be together,' Harry replies as he kisses Bernadette's elbow. Unconventional this may be, but the look of contentment on Bernadette's face says it all.

'Dad, can we go back to all the supermarkets?'

'Why?'

'I want you to get loads of pork pies.'

'Why?'

'Cos I want to get married again this week and can't be arsed to wait another one thousand, one hundred and sixty-two days.'

'What are you saying?' I ask.

'I want to get married this week.'

'Well shouldn't you ask Bernadette?'

Harry turns around to his fiancée. 'I did a bit of a fuck-up last week cos my stomach was queasy and I kept shitting myself, but I don't think I'm going to be shitting myself now so I want to marry you in that decrepit religious building. Is that OK with you?'

'Yes, yes, yes,' Bernadette replies, as she engulfs Harry and continuously kisses the top of his head.

Although that wasn't the most romantic of proposals that I've ever heard it didn't seem to bother Bernadette, who is now crying.

'Did my head hurt your lips?' A confused Harry asks.

'No, I'm just happy.'

Harry nods but clearly doesn't understand.

'What made you change your mind?' I ask.

'Because my arse doesn't feel like going for a shit when I think about getting married.'

The perfect advertisement for marriage.

'Bernadette, I'm sorry I messed up our wedding day last week because of my shits. I should've married you even if I puked all over your wedding dress. You're spectacular, especially your eyebrows and ears. You're the best friend I've ever had.'

Bernadette starts crying. 'Thanks for saying those lovely words about my eyebrows.'

I ring Laura. 'You're not going to believe this but Harry wants to get married as soon as possible.'

'Wow, how did that happen?'

'I don't quite know myself but he's keen to get stacked up on pork pies so we're on our way to do the supermarket tour again. I feel so happy I'm going to buy every pork pie I can lay my hands on.'

'You don't think he'll have second thoughts again?'

'He just told me that the thought of getting married doesn't want to make him go for a shit anymore, so that's the true test. Look I better go as we're crossing the road and I've got to keep my eye on them. I'll ring Alice in a minute.'

'No need, she's right next to me and is already crying.'

'Hopefully it's tears of joy.'

We hit all the supermarkets and pick up thirty-eight pork pies. If this is Harry's safety blanket then it's worth the expense and then some.

We all meet up at a pub a few minutes' walk from the hotel. It's a joyous gathering with all the adults hugging each other while Harry and Bernadette are busy sorting out the pork pies by their expiry date.

'Before I contact Father Quinlan are you absolutely sure about this, Harry?' I ask.

'Yes, I haven't gone for a shit for thirteen hours and forty-three minutes, so I've passed the wedding exam.'

'I don't think he'll be happy if we cancel it a second time.'

'I know that Bernadette doesn't like Adam West but we talked about this on the car journey here and I agreed to only watch the Batman TV series when she's asleep, so everything's OK now.'

Not going for a shit and watching Batman in the wee small hours only are seemingly the perfect reasons for deciding to get married.

'Are you sure?'

'I love her and I always will.'

I've never heard Harry say that before and that statement is enough for me to immediately pick up the phone to ring Father Quinlan, who is delighted to hear our news and has agreed to marry them tomorrow at three o'clock.

'We only want you three, that Greg bloke and the leprechaun to come to the religious building. I don't want any of the Guinness people and all those McCarthy zombies. They're scary and look like their eyes are going to fall off their faces.'

I presume he's talking about my elderly aunts and uncles.

'Can I run down that religious gangway?' Bernadette asks.

'No, you're going to walk down the church aisle slowly. It's traditional to do it that way,' Alice replies.

'That's just dull and boring.'

And there I was thinking that the bride walking down the aisle was the emotional highlight of any wedding day.

I contact the same restaurant that I had originally booked for the reception and informed them that the booking is back on, although only for seven guests as opposed to fifty-eight.

So after a couple of quick phone calls the wedding is going ahead. I can't believe it. The anxiety of the wedding cancellation has been replaced by a feeling of pure happiness. In a few short hours my son is going to get married.

'I think this calls for champagne,' I announce to the group.

'Can I just have a Sprite but without the ice? I hate the noise the ice cubes make when I crunch them. But I have to crunch them cos I don't want them just hanging around in the glass when I've finished my drink,' Harry proclaims.

'And I don't want to be in the room when you open up the bottle of champagne. I hate the noise and I've no idea where that cork is going to land or whether it kills anybody,' Bernadette proclaims.

The next few hours are spent drinking champagne and Sprite. We're all talking excitedly about the big day and can't quite get our heads around this sudden turn of events.

Bernadette and Harry want to return to Halifax after the wedding because they want to eat the Halifax Twirls and Mars Bars in all the supermarkets that we visited today. Naturally, they will again give their ratings. I feel another spreadsheet is about to be created. Harry did ask me if chocolate will taste better once he's married.

They both look just about as happy as I've ever seen them. Harry even accompanied Bernadette to the pub garden when we were about to open the champagne. That's true love for you.

Upon her return she did ask if the champagne cork killed anyone.

In all this excitement my thoughts turn to Laura. I am just so delighted to share this joyous evening with her. Her contented expression reminds me of the day we got married. There was around one hundred and twenty guests in that same Streatham church that Harry is going to get married in tomorrow. I will never forget watching her walk down that aisle. She never looked more beautiful. And she didn't run either. All the problems that followed that blissful day are behind us. Her life changed the day she met Sean. They are the perfect match and now she can move to Ireland with a clear conscience knowing that Harry is settled.

I shall miss her.

CHAPTER FORTY-SIX: 1995

'I was surprised to hear from you again,' Carol says as I sit in a chair opposite her.

'Yeah, it's been a while. I just wanted to discuss a few things with you.'

'How's Harry doing?'

'There's definitely an improvement. His obsession with Thomas The Tank Engine has its benefits as he's been reading a lot of Thomas books which has improved his reading skills and his vocabulary.'

'That's great to hear. In what ways do you think his improved vocabulary has helped?'

'What do you mean?'

'Are you having more meaningful discussions with him now?'

'No, not really. He can tell me the storylines of his Thomas books quite clearly but if I ask him how he's feeling today he'll just give me a one word answer, if at all.'

'That's not necessarily an autistic trait. I think you'll find that's common amongst five year olds. Has his aggression decreased?'

'Yes, definitely but I still get a kick in the shins or a head butt a few times a week.'

'And what triggers these attacks?'

'It could be because I turn off the TV when he has to go to bed or it's completely random.'

'And you said on the phone that he's at a special needs pre-school. How's that going?'

'He's been there nearly ten months, which is the longest he's ever stayed at any of the nursery schools. They're really working on behavioural management.'

'Can you give me an example of their techniques with this?'

'They told me after the first couple of weeks of observing Harry that they realised that his lack of social skills leads directly into his disruptive behaviour. They've worked hard trying to help him understand other people's feelings before lashing out and to some extent I think it's working. Although they did say that this lack of empathy will be with Harry for the rest of his life.'

'Yes, that's autism I'm afraid. But it sounds like he's in the right place which must be a relief to you?'

'Yeah, as you know he's been chucked out of four nursery schools so it's just wonderful that he's in a school that tries to understand his behaviour and deal with it in a constructive manner.'

'Is he on medication?'

'Yes, he's been on a low dosage of Ritalin for about a month now. As you know, I was very wary about this as he's only five years old, but after discussing it with my doctor I decided to start it on a trial basis. He told me that if I'm not seeing any benefits Harry can be taken off it without any side effects.'

'Have you seen any impact?'

'Yes, overall he's been a bit calmer and the school have said that he's been more focused.'

'So I'm seeing a much more encouraging picture here. He's in a good school, he's less aggressive, his reading skills have improved, as has his vocabulary; all good developments. What are your concerns?'

'I know that you specialise in child psychology and you've been spot on with all of your diagnosis to date with Harry, but I need your help with Laura.'

'I was just about to ask you about your wife.'

'In a couple of hours Harry and me are meeting up with her for the first time in thirteen months. As you can imagine I'm nervous and don't really know how to approach this.'

'Can you bring me up to date on her health?'

'As you know she had a breakdown in April last year and has had a couple of relapses since then. Her sister was living with her for about a year but she's now on her own and can get by, but from what I gather she's still very fragile. Her sister still visits her regularly though.'

'And what's her relationship with you and Harry?'

'When she came out of hospital the first time she insisted that we move out of our house so we rented a flat nearby. On two separate occasions she blatantly told Harry that he was solely responsible for her illness. I'm not sure how much he took in and I'll probably never know. Apologies if you've heard all this before but you need to know the whole background.'

'Of course, please carry on.'

'The last time we met was so distressing. She was so cruel to Harry. I made my mind then and there that we weren't going to meet up again until she was better.'

'Did she ever apologise for her behaviour?'

'No.'

'So what's prompted the meeting today?'

'She texted me last week and asked to meet up. I spoke to her sister and apparently Laura's feeling somewhat better although her behaviour is unpredictable. I'm apprehensive. I don't want to expose Harry to her nasty accusations again, but she's his mother so I have to give her another chance.'

'Yes of course, and the law is on her side if she ever decided to take this further.'

'I'm well aware of that. Her request came out of nowhere, so I'm very wary. I don't know why she suddenly wants to meet up when she hasn't shown any interest for such a long time, which in itself I find totally baffling. I'm confused and a little scared and that's one of the reasons I contacted you. I just wanted to talk about it to someone who'll have an objective opinion.'

'The Laura that I met was on the verge of the breakdown. She was angry and aggressive so I do know where you're coming from with this. But from what you've told me previously, I understand that before Harry was born her persona was very different. Is that right?'

'Yes, she's a kind person and we got on really well in the first few years of our relationship. I suppose if an outsider compared our personalities they might say that she was more of a worrier than me. She was more stressed out with all the issues that arose when we were buying our house, whereas I took it more in my stride thinking that it'll all come right in the end. But being a worrier isn't a bad personality trait.'

'The fact that she is a worrier was probably one of the factors that lead to her breakdown. She couldn't cope with all of Harry's issues and from my experience in dealing with parents of special needs children this is all too common.'

'But do any of these parents have breakdowns because of this?'

'Absolutely, yes. It's usually the mothers, as generally speaking they carry more of the responsibility but I've seen fathers also hospitalised due to mental health issues. David, I perfectly understand all your concerns right now but try to look at it from a different angle. Harry is in a better place than the last time we met. Of course, there's still many problems and if I'm honest these will be there to a greater or lesser degree for the whole of Harry's life. There's no miracle cure for autism, it's how you manage it. So have you thought that the reason why Laura contacted you was to try and build bridges and make up for all that lost time?'

'Yes I've tried to think that way but the last couple of years, while we were still together, were just so stressful and full of arguments that I can't help but think that today is going to be more of the same.'

'But since April last year she hasn't had to deal with Harry on a daily basis, you have, so at least that stress element has been removed for her. I really don't know how her mental health is right now but I think that you should go to the meeting today with an open mind. You may be surprised.'

'It never occurred to me that there could be a positive outcome to all of this. Thanks for seeing me today and for everything you've done for my family. It's much appreciated.'

'You're more than welcome. I wish you the best of luck not just for this afternoon but for your future with Harry. Take care.'

Two hours later Harry and I arrive at our old house. Although I have the front door key I ring the bell. Technically I still own half of the property but I haven't lived there for around sixteen months. It doesn't feel like my home anymore.

Within seconds Laura answers the door, she must have seen us arriving. She looks much smarter than the last time we met. She's wearing a short sky blue skirt and matching top which shows off her model type figure. She's still a beautiful woman. She's even wearing makeup which she never did in the last year of our relationship.

'Come in,' she says.

We walk past her and into the living-room.

'Drinks?' She asks.

'I've have a beer and Harry a coke please.'

There's an awkward atmosphere between us as if we're strangers but that's to be expected given what's happened in the last couple of years.

She hands over our drinks and sits opposite us. We're in the exact same seating positions as the last time we met. I hope that's the only similarity to that awful day.

'So how are you?' I ask.

'I have good and bad days but overall I'm feeling better.'

'That's encouraging to hear.'

'And how are you, Harry?' Laura inquiries.

Harry sips his coke but doesn't reply.

'Give him time. He's nervous.'

Laura looks at Harry, waiting for a response that doesn't come.

'I was surprised to get your text. Is there anything specific that you want to talk about?'

'I wanted to find out how you were both doing, that's all.'

'As you know Harry's in a SLD school with an autistic unit. He's doing well.'

'Amanda told me that Harry's taking Ritalin. I don't agree with that, he's only five.'

'The hospital and our doctor recommended it. They both sent out all the relevant documentation to you but you didn't respond to anything, therefore I assumed that you weren't in the correct mental state to handle such decision-making and the medical people agreed with me. We couldn't wait forever.'

I try to keep my tone of voice as calm as possible although there's so much more I'd like to say in a more accusing manner but that will be counter-productive.

'Do you really think it's wise giving Ritalin to Harry?'

'Laura, I'm nervous about it as well but it's definitely had a calming influence on him. It's making his life better and mine too. As I've been looking after him on my own, Harry's behaviour affects me a lot more than you right now.'

'And I have no say in all of this?'

'Of course you do, but you had your chance and I didn't hear any objections from you. In fact, until last week you haven't contacted us at all for the last thirteen months so please don't lecture me on my decision-making when you clearly opted out of that,' I reply more harshly than I intended.

'I haven't opened any envelopes for months,' Laura replies.

'Why not?'

'In case they contained bad news.'

'I tried ringing you a few times but you didn't pick up.'

'I'm not answering any calls.'

'Well you should, what if something happened to Harry? You've got to try to get back to a normal life. I'm not saying it's easy but you have no other option.'

'You've no idea what I've been through.'

I want to sympathise with her because her illness sounds horrendous but I've been dealing with Harry on my own for so long now that it's also had an impact on me. My life is completely centred around my son. My work rota is structured in such a way that I drop him off at his school before I go to work and then pick him up early as well. I've had to work reduced hours to make this possible. Of course, that means that I'll receive less wages, which doesn't go far in paying all the bills for two houses as Laura is not currently working. Somehow I've managed to hold it together but for how much longer I just don't know? I want to say all of this to Laura but decide against it. It's pointless because she won't able to help me in any way. All she seems to do is criticise and wallow in self-pity.

'Anyway if you've still got the hospital letters have a read as it clearly explains the pros and cons of taking Ritalin and the reasons why it was recommended for Harry.'

'OK, I'll do that,' she quietly replies.

'I know that this is a stupid question but I presume you still don't want us to move back in?' I ask.

'No I don't.'

'But you're slowly getting better, I can see that for myself. We can help you with your recovery.'

'No you can't, you'll make it worse. If you move back in I'll end up in the hospital again.'

'Why do you say that? I know Harry's issues haven't gone away but he's not as aggressive as before and whatever problems that come up we'll get the school involved and I'm sure that they'll be able to advise us on the correct behavioural management techniques. They're really on the ball.'

'David, they're not miracle workers.'

'So that's it, is it? You're washing your hands of us? Shall I apply for a divorce now then?'

'I don't know what to think. Can we have this discussion somewhere down the line?'

'OK, that sounds fair but my life's on hold right now. I want to know where I stand at some point.'

'Don't worry, I'll let you know.'

I finish my beer and leave half an hour later. Although nothing was resolved it didn't turn into a full blown argument which made a pleasant change. As we were leaving she promised to stay in regular contact with us from now on.

Harry didn't speak the whole time we were there. She did try to kiss him as we were leaving but he avoided her attempt and rushed out to the car. I felt great sympathy for my wife as I saw her pained expression.

It's going to take a lot of time and effort to repair that relationship

CHAPTER FORTY-SEVEN: 2001

Laura slowly made a full recovery and returned to work part time at the local accountant's office.

Our marriage was unofficially over in the year following Laura's breakdown but it took another six years before we actually got divorced.

Laura purchased a flat nearby and Harry and I moved back into our old house.

As part of the divorce settlement I was given sole custody of Harry.

CHAPTER FORTY-EIGHT

'Are you checking out early, sir?' The hotel receptionist asks me as I carry my cases through the hotel lobby.

'No, my son's getting married in London this afternoon but we'll be back tomorrow morning.'

His confused expression is understandable. But then again don't all the wedding parties travel from London to Halifax on the day before the wedding, then return to London on the day of the wedding, only to come back to Halifax the day after the wedding?

'Where's Harry?' I ask Laura.

'He's over there hiding behind the curtains.'

I can see Harry's shoes sticking out of the curtains.

'And why is he doing that?'

'He knows that it's bad luck to see the bride before the wedding.'

I approach Harry's shoes.

'Harry, you can come out now, Alice and Bernadette have just left.'

'Did they see my shoes?' Harrys asks while still hiding.

'No they didn't.'

I wonder if any of the guests have noticed me talking to the hotel lobby curtains?

Eventually Harry reappears.

'Cos if they saw my shoes, I'll have to cancel the wedding again.'

We put our cases in the car and start our journey to Streatham.

'Are you nervous?' I ask my son.

'No shits so far.'

'Well, you don't need to worry about anything today, Harry. Remember I'm your best man and I'll be by your side the whole time.'

'I knew I should've asked Ben Shephard,' Harry replies, shaking his head.

I'll ignore that dig.

'Laura, how are you feeling?'

'I'm still in a state of shock over it all, but excited. Nothing can go wrong now, can it?'

'No, it's all going to be just fine,' I reply, sounding more confident that I actually feel.

'When was the last time you watched *our* wedding video?' I ask her.

'Not since we came back from our honeymoon.'

'Me, neither. Remember the video camera that was used? It was about a foot long.'

'Yeah and the priest told the cameraman to back off as he was practically alongside us when we were saying our vows.'

'It was an amazing day. My second one was a lot more low-key.'

'Does Kerry know that Harry's wedding was called off?'

'No, I didn't tell her. I'm really not bothered whether she knows or not. It's irrelevant. Only a handful of people know about our split but that's probably more to do with the timing of Harry's wedding.'

'Have you thought anymore about going on holiday by yourself? I think it'll do you good.'

'When I got back to the hotel last night I did look at hotels in New York, so that's a possibility. I'm undecided about it. Will I feel like a saddo travelling on my own? I suppose the only way of finding out is actually doing it.'

'Don't forget to put the pork pies in the fridge as soon as we get home. They might melt if we don't,' Harry tells me.

Managing the pork pies has been occupying Harry's thoughts since yesterday. As soon as we arrived back at the hotel last night Harry insisted that the hotel manager himself store all the pork pies in one of the hotel fridges. Harry escorted the manager to the fridge and arranged them by their expiry date.

'Harry, you're getting a little too obsessed with these damn pork pies. We're only going to bring a couple of them for you and Bernadette.'

'I need to bring all thirty-eight of them in case Bernadette and me get really hungry. I think married people eat more food cos they're fatter than single people.'

'David, at this point I'd agree with anything Harry wants. We don't need any hiccups today,' Laura quietly tells me.

'OK, Harry, I'll put the pork pies in the fridge.'

'Good. Now I'm *really* looking forward to getting married.'

Because Bernadette gave Harry half of her Kit Kat it resulted in Harry proposing to her and now the correct handling of the pork pies will ensure that Harry and Bernadette's wedding day is a resounding success. Is that unusual? Of course it isn't, not in the autistic world anyway.

We're back home by eleven – only four hours to go. Now I'm getting nervous. I look over at Harry sitting in the living-room watching Cartoon Network, seemingly without a care in the world. I sit opposite him.

'Are you still OK about the wedding?'

'Yeah, Bernadette didn't see my shoes, so it should be OK. Will that bloke in the black suit be at the religious building again?'

'Of course, he's the priest and he'll be marrying you both.'

'If I ask Bernadette to come over here you could just say that all those religious bits and pieces for the wedding so I won't have to go to that building and not wear a tie. It's all on the internet.'

'No, that doesn't count. It has to be officially done by the priest at the church. Please don't tell me that you're missing *Family Fortunes* again?'

'No, it's *Strike It Lucky*. Michael Barrymore's great. I love his long legs.'

'Just record it.'

'He's much funnier when the programme's live.'

'How do you feel about getting married to Bernadette?'

'She's got lovely long hair but sometimes when I kiss her ears some of her hairs get in my mouth so I have to brush my teeth loads of times to get rid of them. But I'll still keep on kissing her ears.'

'OK, apart from her hair what else do you like about her?'

'She smiles a lot but doesn't laugh. I don't like people laughing cos then I can see their teeth and tongue; that's gross. I did tell her yesterday that if she has to laugh can she wait until I'm asleep and she agreed that it's the right thing to do.'

Is that part of a pre-nuptial agreement?

The next few hours consist of washing our clothes in readiness for our return trip to Halifax, polishing shoes and ironing shirts. By quarter past two we're both suited and booted.

'Are you ready?' I ask my son.

'Can I just watch the first five minutes of *Strike It Lucky*?'

'No, Harry, we've got to get going. We have to arrive at the church before Bernadette.'

'She won't mind. She knows that I love Michael Barrymore and his legs.'

'Come on, let's go.'

The church is a fifteen minute walk away. On the way there I glance at my son. He's a handsome man. He's taller than me, slim with dark brown eyes. He keeps his hair really short as he doesn't like it getting ruffled when it's windy outside. His words, not mine. Unlike me there is no sign of any bald patches.

I've worried about Harry since the day he was born. I suppose you could say that I'm no different from any other parent but due to Harry's autism and all the problems that that entails I've worried more than most. For an early part of his life there was a long period where he was without his mother but it brought us even closer together. From time to time I get anxious about his future and wonder what will happen to him when Laura and me are no longer around. How will he manage? It's a totally different perspective when you're a parent of an autistic child. But on this very special day I must put aside these dark thoughts.

I stop a man in the street and ask him to take a photo of us. I explain that it's Harry's wedding day.

'Are you nervous?' The man asks.

'No shits,' Harry simply replies.

That explains everything.

The church is empty upon our arrival although I didn't expect it to be packed, given that there will only be four other guests, excluding the bride.

Harry looks at his watch. It's fourteen minutes to three.

'What am I going to do for the next fourteen minutes? I could've watched the first half of *Strike It Lucky*.'

Father Quinlan walks towards us carrying his bible.

'And how are you today, Harry?'

'I'm missing *Strike It Lucky* thanks to Dad and he's supposed to be my best man. Do you know Ben Shephard's mobile number?'

I shake my head at Father Quinlan as an indication not to pursue this line of conversation.

'You've got a beautiful day to get married,' he tells Harry.

'No I haven't. I like it when it's pissing down with rain.'

'Harry, please mind your language. Remember you're in church.'

'You're not going to be waffling on and on about bullshit again today are you?' Harry asks the priest.

'No. I'm just saying the wedding Mass as normal.'

'Just keep it snappy and don't tell any jokes. I don't want people laughing.'

'I'll avoid telling my usual repertoire of jokes, just for today,' Father Quinlan replies with a smile, before retreating into the vestry to get ready.

A few minutes later Laura, Sean and Greg arrive.

'Are you alright, Harry?' Laura anxiously inquires.

'Yeah, my arse is OK.'

This seems to reassure my ex-wife.

Father Quinlan comes back out and at exactly three o'clock the organist starts playing *Here Comes The Bride*.

'I can play the piano better than her,' Harry tells the priest.

We turn around and see Bernadette, accompanied by Alice, walking down the aisle. The wedding dress is absolutely stunning and Bernadette looks like the perfect bride. Halfway down the aisle she breaks away from her mother to run towards Harry and engulfs him in a passionate embrace. I immediately start to well up and with a quick glance around me I can see that everyone else is doing the same.

Bernadette got her wish in more ways than one.

Harry cannot stop looking at his beautiful bride. He looks as happy as I've ever seen him. I even think that he's forgotten about the *Strike It Lucky* episode.

The wedding Mass begins and for once Harry is patient and seemingly listening to what the priest is saying, although looking at his confused expression I'm not sure if he understands any of it.

They're holding hands the whole time.

'If anyone here knows any reason why Harry and Bernadette should not be joined in holy matrimony speak now or forever hold your peace,' Father Quinlan announces.

'Yes, yes, yes,' Harry shouts as he gives Bernadette a high five.

'I thought you might like that bit. By the power invested in me I now pronounce you husband and wife. You may kiss the bride.'

Harry kisses his wife, not on the elbow or her ears but on her lips. This brings a round of applause from the five guests and Father Quinlan.

'My ears are hurting, don't clap too loud,' Harry tells us.

Harry accompanies his wife down the church aisle. This time Bernadette doesn't run, she's savouring the moment.

'Congratulations, son, you've made me very proud,' I say as I greet him outside.

'It was nothing,' Harry replies.

There's lots of hugs and kisses all around. The relief that the wedding finally went ahead is visibly evident on the faces of everybody outside the church.

As the wedding was re-arranged so quickly I couldn't get our original photographer so Father Quinlan volunteers to take photos of the wedding party.

'I'm getting into practice for when I meet Tom Hanks,' Harry remarks as he takes several selfies of himself and Bernadette.

I notice that Laura is standing away from the crowd (does six people count as a crowd?) so I approach her.

'Are you OK?' I ask.

'I'm fine. I just never thought that I'd ever see this day.'

'You and me both, but he's found the perfect partner. I just know it'll all work out for them.'

'Yeah, Bernadette's lovely. They're made for each other.'

'Come on, let's join the rest of the group.'

'OK. I'm looking forward to your best man speech. Is it all sorted?'

'I haven't prepared anything as I just thought that Daniel Radcliffe will jet in from New York at the last minute to save the day.'

We arrive at the pub function room a short time later. This room is huge and needed to be to accommodate fifty-eight guests. Now there's plenty of room for the seven of us so Harry doesn't have to hurt his shoulders bumping into people.

The DJ I hired for Saturday wasn't available tonight so I've brought my ipod down. It's got plenty of music on it, although not too much past 1969 which happens to be the same year that the Beatles recorded Ringo Starr's composition *Octopus' Garden*. A song about how an octopus lives in his garden underneath the sea isn't the most obvious choice for the first wedding dance but it's what Harry and Bernadette wanted and that's all that counts. As the song starts, Harry takes Bernadette's hand and leads her onto the spacious dance floor. They have their arms around each other, dancing very slowly and completely out of rhythm to the upbeat song but I don't think they noticed. We're all recording it on our phones and it's a video I'll look back on for the rest of my life.

This time yesterday the wedding was over three years away so it just astounds me that I'm standing here looking at my married son and his bride.

After their dance is over the guests clap and the newly-weds take their customary bow.

'Now I think it's time for the best man's speech,' Laura announces as she hands the glasses of champagne to the adults and Sprite to Harry and Bernadette.

'By my calculations I'm the tenth choice for best man, behind Bruce Forsyth, Lee Mack, Daniel Radcliffe,

Benny Hill, Arthur Ashe, Ringo Starr, Ben Shephard, Susanna Reid and H from Steps. Believe it or not Harry even asked Ringo personally. Three of those on that list are dead and I'm not sure that Susanna Reid qualifies for best man so I'm sceptical why this last lot were even in contention for the role, nevertheless I'm here even though I had to dye my hair to get the part. Although I practically begged Harry to be his best man I feel honoured and very proud. Autism brings so many unique challenges that most of us don't have to face but Harry has overcome so many obstacles in his short life. As we all know he plays the piano beautifully. This isn't by accident. He practices for several hours every day, it's one of his passions. He's also been working for *PriceLess* for nearly fourteen years and is the third longest serving employee there; that's some achievement in itself. His approach to work is slightly different to his colleagues. Sometimes he'll eat the customers food just to make sure it's up to the required standard and occasionally he'll call customers fuckwits, whether they deserve it or not. Most of the time his autism ensures he gets away with it, almost as if it's his superpower. Imagine if everyone here just openly expressed what they were thinking? Well, Harry does that every day, usually without any repercussions. I'd love to do that. I was talking to Laura outside the church and we both said that we can't believe that our son has just got married. We never thought that it would ever happen but then he met the wonderful Bernadette. I remember Harry telling me about a month into their friendship that she was his fourth best friend. It wasn't long before she became number one. Bernadette's father left the family when she was very young and that must've had an impact on her but you wouldn't know it. She's grown up to be an absolutely delightful young lady and completely devoted to Harry. I couldn't wish for a nicer daughter-in-law. I truly mean that. I think I've said enough. I just want to congratulate Harry and Bernadette and wish them lots of happiness for their future together. Here's to the newly-weds,' I say holding up my champagne glass.

'Cheers,' the guests reply before taking a sip of their champagnes and Sprites.

'Too much waffling and Lee Mack would've got much more laughs if he was clean shaven,' Harry proclaims to the wedding party.

We all laugh at this remark but Harry just looks confused.

'Don't spoil my wedding day by laughing.'

This brings even more laughter.

'OK, it's time to put on some music,' I say.

'Only for the singers that are alive. I don't want to dance to anyone who's dead,' Harry responds.

I play the ipod, starting alphabetically by the artists. If there's any *ZZ Top* fans then they're in for a bit of a wait.

Bernadette takes Harry's hand and they immediately dance to Abba's *Dancing Queen*. They are soon joined by the other two couples. Laura beckons me over but I decline. She's probably thinking that I'm feeling the odd one out but tonight I feel at peace. Any worries about my pending divorce can wait. Today is all about Harry and Bernadette.

I take my iPhone out and video the varying dancing skills in front of me and it isn't long before I join them.

The evening passes in a flash. By the end everyone is in high spirits, probably due to the consumption of spirits and the like. Even Harry told me that he's drunk, but I reassured him that he can't be on three cans of Sprite.

'Thanks for a brilliant day, Bernadette. I'll see you in Halifax tomorrow,' Harry tells his wife.

She smiles and kisses him.

'What are you doing?' I ask my son.

'I can't go with her cos Alice and that Greg bloke laugh too much and she doesn't like my wallpaper.'

'But you've just got married.'

'Yeah I know. I remember that religious bloke saying I now pronounce you man and wife.'

'You've got to spend your first night together.'

'No we don't. Bernadette doesn't hate the Halifax hotel wallpaper so we'll do that tomorrow.'

'It's OK, David. Bernadette wants it that way as well.'

Soon afterwards Bernadette, Alice and Greg make their way home.

Just before Sean and Laura get into their taxi Laura approaches Harry.

'I can't tell you how proud I am of you, Harry,' she says, giving him a big hug.

'Can you get me a *Strike It Lucky interactive* DVD game then?'

'I'll order it on Amazon as soon as I get home.'

'Wow, that will be my favourite wedding present ever.'

Even better than my nine hundred and ninety-nine pounds piano?

Harry then kisses the back of Laura's neck. This is a significant moment as he's never, in his near thirty years, ever kissed either myself or Laura willingly. She looks astonished and starts to cry.

'Did I hurt your neck?' Harry asks.

'No, you didn't. I'm just so happy.'

Harry looks perplexed.

'Come on, Laura, the taxi's waiting,' Sean quietly informs her.

'The perfect end to the perfect day,' Laura tells me as she kisses me and tearfully gets into the taxi.

Half an hour later we're back home. I must admit that despite Alice and Greg's 'constant laughter' (the evil bastards) I still thought that Harry would have changed his mind and stayed at Bernadette's house tonight. I was wrong.

'How does it feel to be married?'

'I feel like one of those happy people. I'm going to be smiling forever, but I won't laugh though.'

Smiling through life. I like that.

'Mum was so pleased that you gave her a kiss without her asking for one.'

'She's buggering off to Ireland soon isn't she?'

'Yes, but not for a few months.'

'So it was a wasted kiss then?'

'No, rest assured it definitely wasn't. Anyway, it's time you went to bed, you've got to get up early tomorrow.'

'When we get to Halifax I'm going to tell Bernadette that I'm going to tear down my Thomas wallpaper so she can stay here some weekends.'

'But you love your Thomas wallpaper don't you?'

'Yes, but I love Bernadette more. Plus she said it'll be much easier sleeping here now your grey hair has vanished.'

Another hair fanatic? Looks like I'll have to stock up on hair dye.

'Bernadette's father didn't bother coming today. He must be a bit of a bastard.'

Good point.

'She said that when her father pissed off her mother was sad for years.'

'I know but she has Greg now and he's a nice guy.'

'Has that Irish chick disappeared forever?'

'I think so.'

'Are you going to be sad for years?'

'I hope not.'

He leans forward and kisses me on my forehead before heading upstairs to his bedroom.

Two voluntary kisses from Harry on the day he got married. It really was the perfect day.

THE END

Lightning Source UK Ltd.
Milton Keynes UK
UKHW010728140221
378748UK00001B/56

9 781839 754418